LIFE –
A FIFTY-FIFTY PATH?

'I believe that it is probably true that fortune is the arbiter of half the things we do, leaving the other half or so to be controlled by ourselves.'

Niccolo Machiavelli, *The Prince,* Chapter XXV

'Always trust your Gut. Your Brain can be fooled and your Heart is an idiot. But your Gut does not lie.'

Anon

LIFE –
A FIFTY-FIFTY PATH?

A Novella

JOHN KIRKALDY

Published by Kirkaldy Press

A CIP catalogue record for this book is available from the British Library.

ISBN 978-1-0685000-0-8

Book layout by Clare Brayshaw

Prepared and printed by:

York Publishing Services Ltd
64 Hallfield Road
Layerthorpe
York YO31 7ZQ

Tel: 01904 431213

Website: www.yps-publishing.co.uk

Dedicated to my five grandchildren –
hoping you will have a great future.

PART ONE

Treading Water

CHAPTER ONE

GOLD FLAKE

Monday, 24th September 2007

Luke Sheppard turned the sack upside down and shook it. He gazed at the Gold Flake cigarette packet that had just fallen from it and read the inscription on the inside.

FOR LUKE – REMEMBER – LOVE JULIE X

Sweetest love, I do not goe
For Weariness of thee,
Nor in hope the world can show
A fitter love for mee; John Donne
Woolgoolga has everything except sand flies

He had last seen the sack at the end of his final term at university, when he had dumped it at home and then had forgotten completely all about it. He smiled as he remembered that his parents had given him the sack of King Edward potatoes for his new flat. He and his three flat mates at Boars Hill had largely existed for nearly a term on every kind of potato dish known to man: baked, boiled, fried, mashed and, inevitably, Shepherd's Pie.

He had shoved all the debris of university life into it for two years: bills, invitations, copies of *Private Eye,* an old driving licence, receipts, post cards ('Dubrovnik is fab – Communism works') and a whole range of miscellaneous junk, ranging from marbles to an out-of-date guide to the London Underground, showing which carriage to get in for a quick exit. What he most remembered immediately was bringing the potatoes back in the train. The carriage had stopped suddenly near Didcot and the potatoes in the rack had spewed out all over the compartment, scoring direct hits on several peevish Sunday evening heads. In the subsequent chaos, he and one of his flat mates, Henry, had got an unstoppable attack of the giggles.

His mother would have approved of the funeral – neat, tidy and organised. She had moved to the bungalow two years ago after the death of his father. (There were no other children; Luke was adopted.) The vicar had struck just the right note, all had agreed, over Harvey's Bristol Cream in the Church Hall: 'Everybody's Friend and Nobody's Enemy.' Oxfam had taken the furniture and clothes, and Mrs Moody, the daily, the dining room table. 'After all, I've polished it often enough.' In the morning, as a last rite, the Council would take the remaining bed. Luke had given the sack one more shake and out then fell the Gold Flake cigarette packet.

Everybody in those days seemed to smoke, especially students; it was a rite of passage. The very poor smoked Number 10 and the slightly better off, Number 6; some even smoked Woodbines. The better off smoked Embassy and collected vouchers. Those striving to be fashionable smoked a weird array; one of Luke' s girl friends had even smoked Balkan Sobranie and had changed its different colours to match her tights. Luke himself had smoked Gold Flake, as nobody else did, and its package was in colours he liked,

Orange and Yellow. If you wished to show solidarity with the workers, you rolled your own. He had found the sack by chance in a cavity in the ceiling that he forgotten.

At once his mind skipped back to October 1968 and an Australian girl, called Julie.

CHAPTER TWO

THE RENT PARTY

Sunday, 27th October 1968

Every student year has *the* party. The party that gets better in the telling. The party that everybody went to, even though not everyone was there. The Rent Party of Sunday, 27th October 1968 is still talked about. Somebody – many could not quite remember who – was giving a party in Kensington (students still lived in Kensington in those days). The idea was that everybody should bring a ten-shilling note. A bottle would also be very welcome. The flat was way behind on the rent and desperate measures were called for. The crowd was enormous and at about one in the morning, the police arrived, thanks to complaints about the noise; at the same time, the ceiling in the sitting room developed a large hole, due to the weight and enthusiasm of revellers above. The tenants were evicted and made most of the dailies next day.

Sunday, 27th October was not only the day of the Rent Party but also of the Vietnam Demo (everybody was retrospectively there as well). Luke had travelled up in the morning crammed into his green Morris 1000 Station Wagon with two others. He had come with Emma, a first year History Student from St Hugh's. She had been impressed initially by his second-year public school confidence, but she was pretty and bright, and had soon worked out that with a male / female ratio of nine to one: 'A girl does not really have to buy dinner much around here.' Somewhere on the A40, the car radio played, *You've Lost That Loving Feeling*. Gary, the other passenger, had a pile of leaflets from the Socialist Society, oozed radical chic from every pore of his donkey jacket. Luke felt on the way out.

They parked the car in Gray's Inn Fields and headed for the LSE. The students had taken over the buildings for the weekend and were organising an illegal sit in on Vietnam. Some 2000 had spent Saturday night there. Two large banners were on the front portal. 'Victory to the Vietnamese Revolution' and 'Adams Closed it. We Opened it.' Occasional chants rang out, 'Hey, Hey LBJ, How Many Kids Have You Killed Today?' and ' Workers and Students United, Will Never Be Defeated.' Luke found himself at one moment listening to a discussion on whether the Soviet Union was a deformed workers' state or simply a capitalist one. There was evidence too of the French influence. 'It's Forbidden to Forbid' and 'Take Our Desires for Realities.' Supporters of Anarchism, Socialism, Communism and Agit Prop argued and debated, fuelled by a heady mixture of coffee, beer and the odd joint. The atmosphere seemed like a mixture of party, revivalist meeting and picnic.

The sit-in flooded down the Strand in the early afternoon towards Trafalgar Square, gathering speed and numbers as it did so. Rumours were everywhere. How many were there on the demo? Some said 100,000; others 200,000; probably in reality, more like 10,000. Tariq Ali and Vanessa Redgrave were *definitely* there. Every protest group seemed to be represented: 'Save Biafra;' 'Free Greece;' and 'Victory to the Engineers.' Somebody had glimpsed Mick Jagger. It was said that US Marines with machine guns (or was it with smoke bombs?) were in the American Embassy. How many police were there? Some said 1000. Others, 2000. The man next to Luke claimed to have seen 'masses' of police dogs and horses. As they passed the Australian High Commission; its flag was burned in protest. Nearing Trafalgar Square, the noise grew ever louder and more deafening. Chants grew faster. Yells of support and abuse came from all sides of the road. Luke remembered one man, puce with rage, screaming at the top of his voice, 'Bastards, bastards, fuck off and get a job. You lazy cunts.'

The speeches in Trafalgar Square were, if the truth were known, something of a disappointment. The well-rehearsed sound bites boomed out across the Square and got the predicable applause at the appropriate places. The same things had been said at similar demos and in numerous student unions for many months. Luke felt confused. He did not believe that America should be in Vietnam, but did not think that Communism was the answer either. 'Typical liberal – stand in the middle of the road and you get run over,' commented Gary; a not very original stab but an effective one. His feelings for him were not enhanced by the sight of Gary and Emma holding hands.

Towards the end, Luke began to understand the power of a mob. A group near to him, claiming to be from the Merseyside Anarchists (a Scouse accent was very fashionable) began to surge down the club land of Pall Mall, turning up St James's Street towards Grosvenor Square. 'Ho, Ho, Ho, Chi Minh, Ho, Ho, Ho, Chi Minh,' the protesters roared and moved forward like a jerky caterpillar at an ever-faster rate. They were joined by other groups proclaiming themselves Maoists, Young Communists, members of the Vietnam Solidarity Committee. But many others, like him, were just swept along, as they sped through the largely deserted streets of Mayfair. Somewhere along the line, Luke gained a banner, which proclaimed, 'US MURDERS PEASANTS – GET OUT OF VIENTNAM NOW.' It featured a napalmed mother and child cowering in a paddy field.

The crowd advanced into Grosvenor Square and towards the American Embassy to be confronted by a wall of policemen and several police horses. If 1848 was the Year of Revolutions; then 1968 was the Year of Demonstrations. All over the world – US, Mexico, Berlin, Northern Ireland, Czechoslovakia and seemingly every other place in the global village – there were demonstrations. The events in May in France set the benchmark. Students and workers had come near to toppling de Gaulle and the Fifth Republic. By October everybody knew their role and what they were expected to do. This was the first media savvy generation of young people. The TV and press cameras waited and were not disappointed.

'Ho, Ho, Ho, Chi Minh' was still the battle cry, as the first wave broke against the police outside the Embassy. The police linked arms and moved forward. For a split second there was a standoff and then a demented battle. Luke froze for a moment and then was sucked into the fray. Firecrackers, smoke bombs and stones were thrown. He tried to use his banner as a weapon but it broke in two. A well-aimed brick hit a policeman. There was a vicious cheer. Scuffles and fights broke out all around him. A massive revenge attack of kicks broke out on all sides as more people went down on the ground. A woman in a red CND sweater with blood streaming down her face, was screaming uncontrollably. The police pressed forward and the demonstrators retreated, linked arms and regrouped.

For Luke the end to the demonstration happened quite dramatically. A large stone, thrown from behind, hit him on the back of his head. He went down and got a kick in the stomach that winded him. His assailant, a large policeman, punched him several times. On all fours, Luke struggled towards the rear, dripping blood. He walked for some time in a daze; caught the Tube; and then watched the news on the TV in a pub off Oxford Street. The demonstrators in the Square had nearly broken the Police but they had held. Most of the demonstrators elsewhere had dispersed peacefully. The battle in the Square lasted for about three hours. Over a pint, his head throbbing, Luke vowed that this would be his last demonstration. He looked in the mirror in the Gents. His lip was swollen; his right eye was coming up in multi-coloured bruising and there were several cuts on his face. 'Not a pretty sight,' he thought as he was sick into the basin.

He would not have gone to the party if had not been for the others. He arrived very late after several more beers and feeling a little drunk. His head throbbed and his face ached. The music was deafening and conversation difficult. *I Can't Get No Satisfaction* was blasting out as he came in the door. He saw Emma and for a moment thought that his wounds might get a vote of sympathy. 'Guess, what?' she enthused, 'Gary has been arrested.' Her wide eyes told him that no cuts or bruises could compete with a prison visit and a court appearance. She was off to see the martyr; no luck there.

He was about to go, when an Australian voice said in his ear, 'Dance with me.' It was a slow number. Many years later a university colleague said that he still got an erection every time he heard Francoise Hardy singing *Tous Les Garcons et Les Filles*. She was tall, blonde and athletic. They wrapped themselves around each other. After a few seconds, they kissed. After a few seconds more, they kissed passionately.

She smelt of Channel No 5 and tasted of cigarettes and beer. 'Take me somewhere.' They stumbled down the stairs and into the car. He had a feeling of guilt about the others for a moment. 'Fuck, two timing Emma' and the People's Martyr, Gary. His headache had gone. They drove, going nowhere in particular, kissing at traffic lights.

'Where are you taking me?'

Luke looked up and saw a sign for the A23. 'Brighton,' he said.

CHAPTER THREE

AN INSANE IDEA?

Friday, 28th September 2007

Thirty-nine years later, Luke met his old flat mate, Henry, for lunch in Ye Old White Horse Pub, in a small alleyway near the LSE. It had been a hastily arranged meeting and was just around the corner from Henry's chambers. University life had changed. There was a sign in the bar saying, 'No Students.'

'Do they rip the place up?' asked Luke.

'No, they just sit in here and nurse a coffee for hours. This is a drinking pub.' He thought for a moment how lucky he was to have left university with no student loan debts.

It was superficially a pleasant meeting and they enjoyed catching up. They had kept up with each other and Luke was the godfather to Henry's eldest son. There was, however, an underlying tension. Henry had moved up and was now very successful. He was one of Britain's top commercial barristers, earning colossal fees. His well-cut suit made the point. Initially, Luke had been successful as a university lecturer but his career at stalled in mid-flight.

Henry had met his wife, Amelia, in Fresher's Week and by Christmas, they were a firm item. They had married the week after graduation. Amelia was now a GP and they had three seemingly immaculate children. They had a house in Islington, a villa on the French / Spanish border and a country cottage in Cornwall. Luke had a modest house, two divorces and no children. Both had got firsts but Luke had sweated through a do or die *viva*; Henry's was the best of his year and all the meeting did was to congratulate him.

'Look, I've got to get back soon, what's really on your mind? Last time we arranged a quick lunch, you were in the middle of a divorce. I can see something's bothering you.' Henry drained the last of his pint.

Then it all tumbled out. Henry listened attentively, asking a few questions as they went along. Luke could see yet again why he was so good in his profession. 'I want to find out what happened to her when she went back to Australia,' he ended lamely. Over coffee in a firm but friendly fashion, Henry urged Luke to forget the whole thing.

From: Henry Norris

To: Luke Sheppard

Date: 28 Sept 2007, 1834

Topic: Totally and utterly insane idea

Luke, you are my oldest friend, but you caught me totally by surprise, I have given this Julie idea some thought. You are a bright guy, although sometimes given to impulsive decisions; this is a totally and utterly insane idea. It is the ultimate lose/lose situation.

Most men by about the age of 12 work out that one of the key steps in getting on with women is to find out their full name. This, despite some great sex and a meeting of minds, you neglected to do. Wandering around Australia, calling out 'Julie', is not a great idea and likely to bring much ridicule.

But let's suppose that you do find her. She is probably now a grandmother with tits down to her waist. She has probably forgotten all about you. Or perhaps she still has visions of those sexy few days, as she heads for her weekly bridge party. You've kept your hair but you're not that gallant young romantic that whisked her off to Brighton.

And supposing she has a husband? What's going to be your opening line, as he meets you at the front door? 'Good day, mate, I shagged your wife nearly 40 years ago.' The Body Line cricket series of 1932 is likely to be a mere nothing in comparison.

I urge you to put this behind you. It is a symptom of boredom and unease. The divorce from Wendy has hurt you. Come down and stay with us. Amelia has given us special dispensation to go down the pub and get drunk.

Key message: Totally and utterly insane idea.

Love and best wishes, Henry

P.S. Amelia sends her love and a kiss. She agrees with the above – 100%.

P.P.S. If you are thinking of doing this, try Roger Smythe, that guy who dropped out after a year to become a photographer. He is in the phone book. By the way, you never thanked me for taking those passengers of yours back to Oxford.

Monday, 1st October 2007

Battersea had changed since he had lived in London doing a PhD in the early 70s, thought Luke. It had, even off and on, elected a Conservative MP. Commuters at bus stops were sometimes seen reading the *Financial Times*. 'Of course, he remembered Luke,' said Roger uncertainly. The mention of the Rent Party, however, did the trick. 'My big break, sold a whole lot of stuff to Fleet Street. Made a few bob. Come round for a drink at lunch and we can do a rummage.'

They climbed the stairs to the attic – almost certainly the servants' quarters in Victorian times. Everything was done in white. Fashion mags would say that the taste was 'exquisite';

Luke was not impressed. 'It would be very difficult to relax around here.' A big cardboard box was lifted down and a brown envelope selected.

'Here we are, the Rent Party. I'd done a lot for *Isis* and *Cherwell* and thought that they would like some pictures. The police, the landlord and the hole in the floor made great images. It was even better that it was just after the Demo. Stayed up most of the night developing them at a mate's and did the rounds of Fleet Street next day. Sold them to four nationals and the *Evening Standard*. Passed Prelims but frankly reading *Sir Gawain and the Green Knight*, and *Beowulf* bored the arse off me. Came up to London and got an apprenticeship. Never looked back.' If not quite in the David Bailey league, Roger had indeed done very well.

'Here,' he said, 'have a look at these, while I get us a glass of wine.'

Luke spread them out on the table. Fashion had undergone a revolution in the late-60s. In the early-60s, students often sported college scarves. In the mid-60s, pop groups still wore jackets and ties. Hair was now longer and skirts shorter. Very few, even at Oxford, wore ties. (The difference, thought Luke, was symbolised in the difference between the Beatles first LP, *Please Please Me*, and *Sergeant Pepper*). He recognised some faces; there was one of Henry and Amelia dancing. There were none of him but four from the end, he came across what he was looking for; leaning against the mantelpiece, looking rather drunk, dressed in a red mini skirt, and clutching a pint mug was Julie. 'Striking girl,' said Roger appearing with a glass of claret. 'Wonder whatever happened to her?'

Monday, 28th October 1968

'Hi I'm Luke'

'Hi I'm Julie'

They both laughed. They had just made love in a lay-by, outside Sayers Cross ('Christ, you Poms have some bloody peculiar names'). It was something of a fiasco but it did not matter. If you are over six foot and must negotiate a gear lever; life can be difficult. Getting her tights off was not that easy either. In the middle he got an attack of cramp. 'God, that's agony,' he yelped.

'Shit, that's the nicest thing that any bloke has said to me.'

They had talked nonstop all the way and even sung a couple of songs very out of tune. They smoked some cigarettes and her lighting his and taking the first few puffs was almost as sexy as kissing her. For the first time in his life, he understood the meaning of the cliché, 'We just clicked.' There are certain situations, Luke thought, where social formalities do not apply: a life raft, going over the top and being stuck in a lift came immediately to mind. It helped that they were both rather drunk and the bottle of wine and some whisky that Luke had liberated on their way out fortified this situation with the odd tot. She was direct in a very Australian way. 'Do you know why I'm here?'

'My classical good looks?'

'You're joking mate, although with all those cuts and bruises, you do look like something of a pirate. No, it's that book of poems in your coat pocket and this is my last weekend before going home. Read me something.' He had brought it along to impress Emma. He read her Andrew Marvel's, *To His Coy Mistress:*

'Had we world enough, and time,
This coyness, Lady, were no crime.'

She laughed. 'You know more women have been seduced by that poem than any other? Look you need to know that I'm leaving for Australia on Thursday afternoon.'

'So, what are we going to do now?'

'I'm starving. I think you should be a gentleman and buy me breakfast and then if you are up for it, we need to find a hotel, so that you can read me some more poems. And you need to buy some Durex; I am regular and this is a good time of the month but we shouldn't be taking chances.'

The car trundled into Brighton as dawn was breaking. They stopped at a newsagent and bought two papers to read about the demo and at a chemist for some condoms. They found a cafe and ordered a full English; nothing prissy about this lady. Emma had the irritating habit of ordering very little food and then making woodpecker like darts at his plate. 'God, you're famous,' she waved the *Daily Express*. Both papers contained a picture of Luke, standing on the outside of the demo, face bleeding, still holding his banner.

'Bugger, that's not going to go down well at home.'

They sobered up and made plans. 'Look, I've got some money and a cheque book, and my rugby kit bag that will convince them that we are not doing a one-night stand.'

'We are having a three-night stand, 'she corrected him, 'and don't worry, I've got some money as well. I will need a ring though (unmarried couples still signed hotel registers as Mr and Mrs Smith). We need to smarten you up a little.' She dabbed at his face with a handkerchief. Luke liked the feminine concern.

They passed an antique shop and he got a cheap ring for £2. He made a quick phone call, shovelling the coins in and nearly forgetting to press button A. 'Henry, this is Luke, listen, something has cropped up. I'm not coming back for several days. Put that essay of mine on Metternich's foreign policy on Dr Smallman's desk and leave a note to say I'm ill or gone home for an emergency or something.'

'What's going on? Where are you?'

'Look, this is a bad line and I'm running out of money. Don't fail me. OK?'

So, they checked into Royal Albion Hotel on the sea front, near the pier. Luke signed the register as Mr and Mrs John Marvel, Donne Street, Oxford. There were few people around and their room was available immediately.

CHAPTER FOUR

LEAVING ON A JET PLANE

Monday, 28th October – Thursday, 31st October 1968

Luke awoke to the sound of seagulls. Early afternoon sunlight streamed through the window. Around the room lay piles of clothes, bottles, cups, a sports bag and the bedspread, thrown off, unneeded. He had woken up a few times after a one-night stand but this seemed entirely different. Then, it had been a case of averting gazes as the other person got dressed; a quick exchange of phone numbers; and a hasty retreat down a flat or college staircase.

He studied Julie closely as she slept – tall (five nine?) with blonde hair, but the adjective that most came to mind was strong. He drifted back to sleep with a smile on his face.

Luke woke again to a sharp kick. Julie had got up, tided the room and was now stretched out, leaning on her elbow. 'Tell me about yourself.'

'No, you.'

'Toss you for it.' He felt into his trouser pocket by the bed and found a coin. He lost the toss and started to describe his upbringing. It was not till then that he fully realised how strange an upper middle class English background really was. He explained about nanny, whom he saw more of than his parents. He ate his meals with her and the cook in the kitchen till he was deemed to have sufficient manners.

'Christ you, Poms are snobs.' Julie was amazed that his parents had sent him away when he was eight to board at prep school. 'Jeez, that's barbaric.'

Luke told how that at no-one anyone called anybody by their first name and in the first year, they were only referred to by a number (his was 28). He described the fear of being beaten – a regular occurrence. He did not describe the awful food, the cold and the sadness of the school train from Paddington. He had blotted out the occasional wet bed and the heavily censored letter home ('I don't think, your parents really want to know that, Sheppard.')

'Weren't you unhappy?'

'Not really, it was standard at that time. I was good at sport and at lessons. I was good at fighting; that was very important. I did write home to ask to be taken away once and sneaked out and posted it.'

'What happened?'

'My mother sent me a plane kit. We did have some fun. We made camps. Played cowboys and Indians.'

'My mother advised me about men,' Julie explained. 'Never marry a man that does not have calluses on his hand.' She described a life in a property in the outback of Queensland with an unpronounceable name; a background of seven fat years and seven lean years – of drought and good times. At one time, things were so bad that her grandfather didn't have enough cartridges to shoot the cattle that were dying for lack of anything to eat.

'And the bloody rabbits!' Luke had visions of fluffy bunnies from children's stories. Julie shook her head. 'You're joking. They would eat you out of house and home. Bastards.'

They made love again – slowly and much more confidently.

Luke realised that this was the first time of being in an equal sexual relationship. If he was honest, he knew very little about women. He had no sister or close female relatives. Eleven years of all male boarding schools had not helped. Even Oxford was mainly male with women incarcerated in single-sex virtual nunneries with strict visiting rules.

Let's make a deal,' he said, as she lay in the crook of his arm. She smelt of soap and wine, and he realised that he had not washed yet. 'We've got very little time. So why don't we take it in turn to make decisions?'

'OK, toss.' Luke won.

'Tonight, we will go swimming and make a bonfire on the beach. We can cook something.'

'You must be nuts. We've no cosies and it's freezing.'

'My decision, remember.'

'OK but it's my turn. We don't say what our surnames are. In any case, I feel that I am Julie Marvel.'

They packed his rugby bag with blankets, tooth mugs and towels from the hotel, along with his sweater, team shirt and socks. They 'borrowed' some cutlery as they went through the dining room. On the way they bought some sausages, bread, butter, mustard and cheese. They still had enough whisky and wine but got some beers, 'just in case.' The size of an English steak provoked derision. 'Cripes, we wouldn't feed that to our dogs back home.'

They drove west along the coast road. It was a balmy evening and the stars were out. It was near to perfect as you could get. The gibbous moon was reflected on the sea. They drove through towns and villages until they got to Littlehampton and, for no real reason, turned into the town and took the signs to the beach.

'This is so different to Australia. It's beautiful,' said Julie, adding 'the bush is beautiful too but it's cruel. You can die in the bush.'

They lugged the kit down to the beach and found some drift wood. They made a fire and put part of an old wire fence on top. Luke stamped on it to make it flat. His efforts at fire lighting were brushed aside.

'Give it to me, you wouldn't last two minutes in the bush,' laughed Julie.

'I will have you know; I got a fire lighter's badge in the Cubs.'

Julie snorted, 'They must have given them away.' As she spoke, the fire took hold.

Male pride raised its head. 'Get your clothes off! Last one in's a sissy.' He should have known that offering a sporting challenge in an English accent to any self-respecting Aussie was fatal. She shot past him and he was just able to catch her hand. They stumbled into the water together, laughing and screaming. He could see that she was a good swimmer. He splashed her; she ducked him with a firm grip. They cried out in glee at the coldness of the water, then raced back to the fire.

'Julie, I can't believe this,' said Luke, a roll in one hand and a large glass of red wine in the other. She looked gorgeous (that was the only word he could think of), wearing his rugby shirt, shorts and socks with a woollen hat.

'You only like me for the rugby gear. Read me a poem,' said Julie lightly.

In the circumstances, there was only one that he really could read: Matthew Arnold's *Dover Beach.*

The sea is calm tonight.
The tide is full, the moon lies fair
Upon the straits; – on the French coast the light
Gleams and is gone; the cliffs of England stand,
Glimmering and vast, out in the tranquil bay.

'That's beautiful, what's it about?'

'There are all kinds of thoughts on that (he did it for A Level). Matthew Arnold was on his honeymoon. Some say he was thinking about the advance of modern science and loss of religious faith. It does not really matter. The best bit is at the end: "Ah, love, let us be true to one another."'

He buried his face in her hair. 'Julie, you're very special.'

'You too' and she nipped his ear.

They piled more wood on the fire and became maudlin.

'Do you ever wonder who your parents were?' asked Julie.

'Very occasionally but not often. My step parents have been very honest with me. I have always known that I was adopted. It's just that they seem rather remote. I have cuddled you more in one day than I have them in a life time. Yet they have always been there for me. What about you?'

'Mum and Dad are OK. The trouble is that they don't really understand me,' Julie sighed. 'There's hardly a book in the place. My passions are poetry and horses. They just want me to marry a grazier.'

'What's the difference between a grazier and a farmer?'

'Acres!'

Julie threw some more wood on the fire and poured them both another drink. It was nearly midnight. 'I want to open a riding school and I know the exact place – Woolgoolga. It's on the New South Wales coast. It's got a beach to die for.'

He toasted them both. 'Here's to Woolgoolga.'

Eventually, they drove back to the hotel. Her head was on his shoulder and for some reason, she did some of the gear changing. It did not work very well but they both thought it hilarious. She had her hand on his prick for some of the time.

'That's very distracting.'

'A good driver is always concentrating, ' she teased.

'Of course.'

They crept into the hotel, using the late key, and collapsed into bed, having first posted the Do Not Disturb sign.

He woke next morning with her whispering in his ear, 'Will you do something for me?'

'Yeah, OK. What do you want me to do – kill a dragon?'

'No, I need a toothbrush, tooth paste, lipstick, nail varnish and some face powder.'

He found the local Boots. When it came to nail varnish, he hesitated: very red (too tarty?) or light pink (too feminine?). He got both and some bubble bath. In the window of the antique shop, where they had bought the ring, he saw a very battered guitar for £5.

He returned in triumph to find her in the bath. He lobbed the entire contents of the bubble bath into the water and bubbles enveloped much of the room. He got into the bath with her. They kissed and then had a bubble fight. 'Do you know what I would like to do now?'

'What? Surprise me.'

'Suck your tits.'

'I would like that.' It led to the inevitable conclusion.

Later he serenaded her from the bath, while she sat on the loo, painting her nails. He was a terrible singer, knowing only three songs – *Michael Row the Boat Ashore, I Walk the Line* and *Summer Time Blues.* Like nearly every other male of his generation, he had sent away a postal order for the *Bert Weedon Play in A Day Guide.* Lack of talent, application and motivation made him a poor master of one and a bit chords. (Being left-handed didn't help.)

I can't believe that I am sitting here, listening to that dreadful racket. What colour would you like my nails?'

'I like both.'

'Right. I'll paint alternate toes and fingers. I'll do you as well.'

Later that day they explored Brighton. They skimmed stones on the beach (where a few years earlier Mods and Rockers had fought pitched battles at Bank Holiday weekends). She was not impressed.

'Do you realise that there are 614,000,000 pebbles on the beach?' Luke asked.

'Not as good as Surfers,' Julie said with disdain, 'not enough sand.'

She loved the Pavilion. 'So, over the top, unbelievable.' Luke was about to launch into a long speech about George IV, when she stopped him. 'Don't spoil it. I love it just as it is.' They ate fish and chips on the pier. They shared a stick of rock. On the way back to the hotel, she bought some jeans. He admired the quick and decisive way she made up her mind as to what she wanted.

'My turn to make a decision,' grinned Julie I want to treat you to an Indian meal. Anything is better than a Pommie steak.'

That night, they lay in a tight ball of sensuality and talked into the early hours of the morning. She told him of a life where you had to drive long distances for most things. Water was incredibly precious. There had been an attack of rats. 'Bloody things ate everything.'

Primary school was fifty miles away and secondary eighty miles. Queensland Uni did not give degrees in partying. 'In any case, Psychology was a waste of time; you spent most of the time analysing the bloody obvious.' Julie quit after a year, just before the exams. 'I want to work with horses; when you're riding, it is like poetry.' Luke remembered that he had sat only once on horse and it was not like poetry, indeed his five-year-old self found it rather scary.

They drifted in and out of sleep. They agreed that they preferred the Stones to the Beatles. Red wine to white. They would never be vegetarians. There was a major disruption when Julie said that her favourite poet was Banjo Patterson. 'Nobody is called Banjo,' declared Luke.

She hit him with the pillow. 'You're talking about the composer of *Waltzing Matilda* – that should be our national anthem. My favourite poem of his is *The Man from Snowy River*; every Aussie kid knows it. It's got my favourite line: "For the bushmen love hard riding where the wild bush horses roam."'

They both agreed that *Dr Zhivago* was one of the best films ever made and peace was restored but they were too tired to think of any others. Luke turned to her in the dark. 'Julie, I'm in love with you.' But she was fast asleep.

Julie always seemed to wake up first. 'We get up at first light.'

Luke groaned at such heartiness. Julie ignored his protest. 'My turn to make a decision. I have never had breakfast in bed. Put on that posh accent and order.' Over a substantial breakfast they planned their day. They drove out along the coast and stopped at the cliffs at Peacehaven. Luke did not want to admit it but he did not have a very good head for heights. They had the cliffs virtually to themselves; an occasional walker passed by, usually with a dog, as they looked out to sea.

'Julie, does this really have to end?' His head was on her lap. She counted a few ships on the horizon.

'Look,' she said, 'this has been a lovely time but it is not life. You are 21 and I am just 22. You are going back to Oxford and I am going back to Australia. That's 14,000 miles.'

'We could write.'

'Like those letters you told me you used to write to girls at other boarding schools. No way. In any case, our worlds are so far apart. You wouldn't last two minutes in the bush. One year of university was enough for me. This has been really good but let's end on a high. Now read me another poem. What about a Shakespeare sonnet?'

'What's your favourite?'

'It has to be 29.'

He read from the anthology:

'When in disgrace with fortune and men's eyes
I all alone beweep my outcast state,'

He read on and she finished it from memory:

'Haply I think on thee, and then my state,
Like to the lark at break of day arising
From sullen earth, sings hymns at heaven's gate;
For thy sweet love remember'd such wealth brings
That then I scorn to change my state with kings.'

Their mood changed and they laughed, when a few minutes later, on cue a lark did emerge and sang.

Where do you want to be in ten years' time?'

'I want to write.' Luke explained how in his opinion history was changing. No longer was it about kings and queens and battles. He told her how at prep school they had to learn dates that did not really mean anything. How at public school, he had come across two inspirational teachers. History was now going to be about ordinary people. They would often be filmed and recorded and have a voice for ever. History was going to connect. 'I am going to dedicate my first book to you.'

'So, my first horse at the riding school has got to be called Luke. Deal?'

'Deal.'

Julie then told him all about her year in Europe. It did not come as any surprise that she had seen more of Britain and Europe than he had. 'What's your favourite place?' he asked.

'It has to be Brighton with Venice as a close second.'

Luke laughed. 'Now listen, it's my shout, I am taking you out to dinner tonight.'

On the way back, he made another phone call to Henry.

'Henry, I will back on Friday.'

'What's going on? Your tutor is on the verge of ringing your parents. Emma has been round twice. Gary has apparently let fame get to his head. The rugby club have rung – can you play Saturday?

'Keep everything on hold, I will be back Friday.'

The choice of venue was an inspiration. The local pub was doing a folk night with an Irish group. Luke and Julie would have been sad left all on their own, instead they sang all the old favourites with gusto: *Whiskey in the Jar, Wild Rover, A Nation Once Again* and *Kevin Barry*. Everybody did a lot of dancing, singing and drinking. Luke did a kind of a fandango with the barmaid and the Charleston with a social worker. They ate steak and ale pie and chips. The landlord bolted the door at closing time and put the empty till on the counter and everybody went on well past midnight.

'Do you realise, that many Australian folk songs are based on Irish ones?' asked Julie.

It was the perfect last night. Julie sang *Click Go the Shears* and Luke sang *Jerusalem* through the empty streets, as they lurched home. 'You are drunk,' he said.

'No, just unsteady on my feet.'

They did not draw the curtain and the moon shone in. Their love making was their most adventurous yet. In the middle, she whispered: ' now you can see now why it is called Down Under'.

As Luke drifted into sleep, he remembered a snatch of the John Denver song, *Leaving On A Jet Plane:* 'I'm leaving on a jet plane, don't know when I will be back again.'

They left early next morning. The weather had turned and it began to drizzle. Conversation grew more stilted. As they approached the lay-by near Sayers Cross, where they had first made love, she said: 'Stop the car. We need to talk. I can't stand all this sentimental crap. Let's end well and no tears and no regrets, OK?'

She kissed him. 'OK?'

'OK.'

'Let's make a joint decision. No long-drawn-out goodbyes. Drop me at the airport and that's it.'

Somehow, the mood lightened a little. He drove to Philbeach Gardens, part of the Australian empire around Earl's Court, so that she could pack up her belongings. She emerged after quarter of an hour with a posse of Australians, who said that they would see her soon, and a suitcase, covered in stickers.

They drove along the M4. He could sense that she was excited to be going home and sad to be leaving. She told him the story of how two of her flat mates had tried the week end before to have a race around the crescent shape of Philbeach Gardens, jumping from car-top to car- top, till one of them fell through the canvas hood of an MGA and got stuck.

They stood in the departure lounge. 'Look, don't wait.'

'Julie, I want you to have something.' He handed her the poetry anthology.

'Give me something to write on. Don't read this till after I'm gone.' He handed her the cigarette packet. She stopped at a table, thought for a moment, and wrote.

Their departure was made worse by the proximity of a man who was obviously emigrating and his mother who was seeing him off. She was being brave, while he kept telling her that she would visit soon; that he would phone often; and it might not be forever. He went through the barrier, waved, and was gone; she broke down and her body convulsed with sobs.

Luke and Julie hugged and then Julie strode off, not looking back.

Of course, Luke disobeyed her. He waited in the departure lounge to see her plane take off. Nearly two hours later, he saw her stride towards the Qantas jet. She got to the top of the aircraft steps and turned round and waved. Bitch! she knew that he would wait. Why was it that women always seemed to be one jump ahead?

Luke could not face the M4, so he took the A4 instead. Somewhere near Reading – he stopped in a lay-bye and in a tribute to Jimi Hendrix, smashed his guitar and burnt it. He could not go any further than Hungerford and booked in at the John O'Gaunt pub. He stayed in the bar drinking Scotch, but however much he drank, he could not get drunk. Finally, he fell asleep and was helped up to his room. Next day, nursing his first real adult hangover, he headed for Oxford.

CHAPTER FIVE

VIEW FROM A WINDOW

Tuesday, 6th November 2007

Luke looked out of the window of his university office. On his desk lay a pile of Year One essays. 'Why,' he thought,' is the School of Architecture nearly always the ugliest building on most campuses?'

He had arrived in the mid-1970s and was still there. It had been easy to get a lectureship then, armed with an Oxford First and an LSE doctorate. Universities were still expanding and student numbers rising, although some of this had been achieved by telling polytechnics to change their letter head.

He longed for a cigarette but a few months before they had been banned from the work place. He reached into his desk drawer and took out the whisky bottle and spiced up his coffee. His smoking was now down to ten a day. He looked again at the picture of Julie at the party and the memories kept coming back to him. Every other moment he remembered another incident or saying.

'God, my choice of poems,' he thought, 'what a cliché. The only excuse is that I was only 20.' At least he had not chosen Elizabeth Browning: 'How do I love thee? Let me count the ways.' That would have been ten out of ten.

'Then,' he thought,' I have not actually looked at or opened a book of poems in thirty years.'

His love of history had dwindled in the early 1990s and had gone into terminal decline by end of that decade. Part of it was the growing realisation that getting a professorship was highly unlikely. He was also disinclined to get heavily involved in academic administration and tried to keep his membership of committees to a minimum.

Part of it was the complications of his private life. He remembered a seminar in north London in the late 70s with various leading historians on why you should study history. After a long discussion the chairman turned to the legendary, A.J.P. Taylor – 'Why should anybody study history?'

'There's only one reason for studying history,' commented Taylor,' because it is interesting.' That was the problem in a nutshell; Luke had lost what the French called the *concierge* mentality, named after the woman at the foyer of many French flats, who knew exactly what was going on in each one. He had forgotten the thrill of finding something unexpected. He remembered being given a World War One diary, kept by a soldier at the front and against all regulations, hidden in a neighbour's desk; unknown for half a century.

He remembered doing the research for his first book on the experiences of soldiers during World War One. He had interviewed a man in his mid-eighties, who had gone over the top with the Hampshire Regiment on 1st. July 1916, aged then just nineteen. He had got two hundred yards, been shot and had lain in No Man's Land all day, listening to the sound of the battle and the dying and wounded. He had been rescued but had a leg amputated and spent two years in hospital. The old man described how his mother had looked out of the window in a working-class suburb of Southampton, watching the delivery of the dreaded telegram. When his mother heard the knock on the door and opened it, she had fainted but later burst into tears of joy, when she read it and found that he had only been wounded.

'She gave thanks to God that I had been spared.' Luke and the veteran had cried together at the thought.

Researching for his next book on Ireland. Luke had come across the register for a west county workhouse during the Great Famine of the 1840s. He looked particularly at the rate of death for children and was appalled by the length of the list of the dead, which stretched over many columns. The causes of death were remorseless – malnutrition, cholera, typhoid, exhaustion, hunger and many more, including measles.

'Measles?' he had asked a doctor friend.

'A real killer, if you have no food in your belly,' was the grim reply. That night, he had put his pub meal into the bin, uneaten.

There were, of course, aspects of the job that he liked. His lectures had always gone well and he had honed them into a professional presentation over the years. He enjoyed running the Year One Aspects of European Civilisation course (nicknamed – Plato to NATO). Last year, a student had a bad attack of flu and missed the entire Middle Ages.

More problematic, and underlining his disenchantment, was the newly introduced third level course on the 1960s. He realised that for the students the 60s were now as distant as the 1930s were for his generation. (His street cred was enhanced slightly by that picture of him at that demo being in one of the set texts.) It is said that if you can remember the 1960s, you were not there. Luke felt the reverse, he felt that, somehow, he was rather stuck there. Little did he realise that when he bought the Kinks' LP that he would be sitting around seriously discussing it, as if it were some kind of work of art. This had led to some awkward moments; last week his tutor group were discussing pop music and whether it could portray serious messages. They all agreed on Bob Dylan. Luke then suggested that Paul Simon was an example of a pop singer, whose lyrics could sometimes be seen in terms of poetry. There was a stunned silence and then one of the brightest, who been getting As or Bs in all her essays, piped up, 'Who is Paul Simon?'

He was becoming cantankerous when it came to spelling and grammar. Verbal and written atrocities confronted him every day. The muddling up of its/it's and there/their. On his desk was a note from one of his students, saying that he could not go to any tutorials on Friday's. (It had come as quite a shock to find, when he was clearing out his mother's bungalow, and came across a lot of his university essays, that he had made most of the same mistakes himself.)

There was one overwhelming image of his present state of mind: Treading Water. But he felt redemption was at hand. Luke had received two letters that week. The first was from his mother's solicitors, saying that her estate had received probate and was worth some £85,000. Her bungalow was on the market at £165,000 and the estate agents were optimistic for a quick sale. The second was from the Vice Chancellor, offering staff generous terms for early retirement. His application letter was written and was sitting on his desk. He was sure that he would post it and that the university would accept it.

PART TWO

Julie

CHAPTER SIX

ARRIVAL

Monday, 15th September 2008

'International travel is absurd,' thought Luke, as he sat in the departure lounge of Singapore Airport. His plane had been delayed for nearly a day and the tape in the lounge was only able to play one tune – *Greensleeves.* He tried – without success – to envisage Henry VIII, the alleged composer, coping with Singapore or a failed tape player. 'A royalties issue,' he guessed.

The world news was grim; the financial crisis was at its peak. Lehman Brothers had just gone bankrupt. However, Luke felt light-hearted. His retirement had gone like clockwork: appropriate words had been said; the dross of thirty years of occupation of his office had been removed (how had he obtained a copy of *An Economic History of Bulgaria,* complete with a picture of Stalin at the front?); departmental and university farewell parties had been weathered; and his house let for six months. He was demob happy.

'Guests are like fish, they go off after three days,' his parents had told him repeatedly. In that time, he did everything that a Sydney tourist should do: swam at Bondi; walked in Centennial Park; took a ferry across the Harbour;

and went on a wine tour of the Hunter Valley. Bearing in mind his parents' saying on his last night, he took his hosts to Doyles on the Rocks for a fish dinner. They drank champagne and looked across the Harbour to the Bridge and the Opera House. 'Here's to Australia,' he toasted. He had come only with a laptop, a small suitcase, a guidebook, a notepad and that photograph.

The next day in the hired car was the worst motoring experience of his life since a very drunk French friend – with Luke as passenger – had tried to negotiate Piccadilly Circus, driving the wrong way round in the Friday rush hour. He had assumed – wrongly – that heading north on the Pacific Highway was easy. The Harbour Bridge looked spectacular but it was confusing with masses of signs to places he had never heard of. He solved the problem by remembering that two Jamaican Prime Ministers had been called Manley (Jamaica had been his last holiday destiny). He followed the signs there and bought a road map. As he drove north, he became more conscious of a mixture of cultures: British – Nelson Bay, Newcastle and Swansea; Aborigine – Cooranbong, Dungog and Bulahdelah; and Australian – Tuncurry, Kempsey and Macksville. The distances involved were vast and the lorries with the lights down the side seemed like dragons in the dark.

CHAPTER SEVEN

WOOLGOOLGA

Friday, 19th September 2008

'Woolgoolga is a town on the Mid North Coast of New South Wales. It is on the Pacific Highway, 550 kms north of Sydney and 400 kms south of Brisbane. The closest city is Coffs Harbour. Woolgoolga has two beaches on the Pacific Ocean. The area has long been a centre of banana growing. Woolgoolga has the largest Sikh/Punjabi population in Australia. *Curryfest* was inaugurated in 2006 to celebrate the culture of the local Sikh community,'

Welcome to Woolgoolga, brochure, 2008

Luke timed his arrival to perfection. Dusk is sudden in Australia. His first sight of Woolgoolga was the lights of the Sikh temple on the hill outside the town. He turned down the road to see a tourist board's delight of a beach; seven miles of perfect sand. A few surfers were still riding the waves. Family groups were packing up and heading for the car park. He could almost smell the BBQs and hear the beer cans being opened. In the middle of the town was something that made him stop, get out and start taking pictures, the second Sikh temple, *Guru Nana Sikh*. It was magnificent and so unexpected: a large white building, guarded by two 'horsemen', with one, what he wanted to call a large 'minaret', dominating the whole building and two more 'minarets' to the side. There were lights through the many windows and umpteen 'minarets' on the roof. It was a bold statement of faith in a most Australian of backgrounds.

He booked in at his B&B and headed off for a steak and a beer. Later, he walked to the Water Tower, the local vantage spot, and looked out across the beach, as the Pacific Ocean pounded in. It was deserted but he seemed to see a lone rider, blonde hair streaming out behind her, riding at full gallop towards the horizon. For the first time in years, he felt the excitement associated with research. Tomorrow, anything was possible.

Saturday, 20th September 2008

Luke ate his breakfast – looking over the beach, dressed in shorts and an open necked cotton shirt. A feeling of smugness emerged from reading the paper. It was raining and 65 degrees Fahrenheit in London, and Australia seemed relatively unscathed in the international financial meltdown. Woolgoolga (he learnt that locals usually called it Woopi) seemed a fascinating social case study – almost 50/50 – Sikh/Non-Sikh. Yet the Sikhs seemed in no way an inferior group. They owned nearly all the surrounding banana plantations, and many had been there for generations and were clearly prosperous. Their strict dress code and manners contrasted with the bikinis, sandals, tee shirts and the whole beach culture. Luke wondered whether it would take several generations for integration to happen, as in other immigrant cultures? Just then a blonde and suntanned surfer passed on his motorbike with a very attractive Sikh girl clinging on behind. They made an incredibly striking couple.

Woolgoolga had changed from Julie's descriptions. It had doubled in size in the last forty years. The sign about the sand flies had long since gone. Houses and real estate were being sold at a rapid rate.

Over his second cup of coffee, Luke made his list and shortly afterwards he set off. It was a dismal day. He trudged between – the police, local newspaper, shops, post office, the rumoured to be the oldest inhabitant, riding school, main restaurants, cafes, and the pub. The dialogue in all of these was almost identical. 'Sorry, mate, never seen her. Friend of yours, is she? Pity you didn't get her surname'. He got some odd looks and a few jokes at his expense. 'What happened, the missus kick you out?'

By evening, he was tired, depressed and footsore. It seemed he gone down a blind alley and Henry had been – as ever – proved right. Luke wondered how much longer he would stay in Australia. He drank a couple of beers in the pub and then headed down to the Gents. Along the darkened walls of the corridors were pictures of local sporting teams – Rugby Union and League, Aussie Rules and Cricket. He was amused at the changes in fashion, especially of hair length.

He stopped in front of some cricket teams and was hit by a literal bolt from the blue: the wild card of wild cards. Sitting at the extreme left in the middle row of the 1969 team was an unmistakeable figure with the score book on her lap and a wide smile. The ID read: 'Julie Colquhoun, scorer.' He'd had, what all researchers need occasionally: a massive stroke of luck.

It was easy to borrow the pub's telephone directory for Queensland. There were four Colquhouns around Longreach and another in Brisbane. The Chairman of the cricket team had been with the team for a long while and lived a few miles out. Luke soon had a phone number.

Luke went back to study the picture and was hit by an even bigger bolt from the blue. The light in the passage was dim and he lit a match. 'Crikey, she has put on weight,' he peered even closer at the picture that had faded somewhat in the light. 'Bloody hell, she has not put on weight, she's pregnant. She is carrying my child.'

CHAPTER EIGHT

QUEENSLAND

Sunday, 21st September – Tuesday, 23rd September 2008

Sleep would not come. Luke tried everything. He wrote notes and tidied his suitcase. It seemed that Julie was alive but, even more amazing, he was a father (or so he assumed). He had always wanted children and now, it seemed, he'd acquired a child in late middle age. He drank some whisky; by morning his bedclothes were in a tight ball at the end of his bed.

Next morning, Luke drove the three miles to see the Chairman of the cricket club, Jack Withall. It became more tropical and humid as he drove inland. Jack was a founder member of the club and, like most veterans, delighted to reminisce; the problem was keeping him on topic. Luke listened politely to the founding of the club, just after the War, the problems of pitch maintenance and the ups and downs of cricket leagues. At long last, he got to the 1969 team. Luke came to the point, 'Do you remember Julie Colquhoun?

'Sure, scored for us for most of the season. Some scandal there I reckon. She would not say who the father was. Family not best pleased. Times were different then and Queensland was very conservative.'

'Where did she live?'

'She did waitressing and lived at one of the cafes – no longer there. Popular, bought her round. Used to ride some horses from one of the fellers in the team.'

By mid-morning, Luke was back at the B&B. He poured himself a large Scotch and ate part of a cheese sandwich. He wrote down the number for the main property near Longreach. He took a deep breath and dialled. The ringing seemed to go on forever.

At long last, an elderly female voice with a very strong Australian accent answered. Luke paused for a second and then plunged right in, 'Hello, I'm a friend of Julie's from England, Luke Sheppard, is she available?'

He heard a sharp intake of breath, a sob and then tears. Eventually, she got out the words, 'you must speak to my husband.'

A much harsher accent followed, 'You have no idea of what grief you have caused. Come here and we can talk.'

'Is it possible to speak to Julie?' demanded Luke.

'No, it's bloody not.' No more details were forthcoming.

Luke left early next morning with his feelings even more confused. Where was Julie? Why such a hostile reaction from her father? Was her child his – the dates certainly fitted? How much – if anything – did any child know about him? He drove along the Pacific Highway, hardly taking note of where he was going. It was getting hotter and he tried distraction from the radio but with no luck. The sight of Surfers' Paradise, near Brisbane, depressed him even more; all neon lights for the usual international takeaways, a kind of tropical Blackpool. Once in Queensland, he joined the Bruce Highway but he was growing so tired that he could hardly think; even signs saying that he was near the Barrier Reef (which he had always wanted to see) could not rouse him. Finally, when he got to Gladstone (how wonderful that the most austere of British Prime Ministers had a town named after him on the Australian coast, offering all kinds of holiday distractions); he collapsed in a road side motel.

Next day he turned inland and found a different Australia. The heat grew more intense and the road narrower, but ran straight for mile after dusty mile. The landscape was bleak- a few trees and bushes. Branches jutting out at awkward angles. Rocks and stones were heaped up in random piles. He saw his first wild kangaroo and was glad of the presence of gallons of water in a container on the backseat and air conditioning. A sign announced that he was now on the Tropic of Capricorn. Ever since he had arrived in Australia, Luke had been searching for a historical parallel. Suddenly, it came to him, Alexis de Tocqueville's first-hand descriptions of early 19th Century America. This French critic admired the vigour of American society and its lack of cant and respect for hierarchy. He predicted that in the 20th Century, America and Russia would be the world's two super powers. How could Australia really miss in the 21st Century: a relatively small but expanding population, every known mineral resource and a society based on a get up and go immigration culture?

Luke stopped at the Wellshot pub in Ilfracombe, some miles short of Longreach. The pub clientele was more than happy to give him directions to 'the Colquhoun place.' He was intrigued to see that in Queensland not only was the beer chilled but also the beer glasses. All round this area were hints of Devon; he had passed through Brixton and Dartmouth, and seen a sign to Devonshire.

The house was at the end of a five miles dirt tract. It was a large, single storey building, made of wood – with a surrounding veranda. Extra parts had been added over the years and the whole thing was built on stilts, a foot off the ground. There were louver windows, and he could see mosquito netting; he imagined some inside rooms would be air conditioned. There were towers for water and oil, and a large tank for petrol. The house was dominated by two large aerials for TV and radio, and the phone. There was a wooden fenced paddock and, in the distance, sheds for machinery.

Luke did not get a warm welcome. Two sheepdogs gave him a very off-hand look before going back to sleep. Julie's father, Eric, was tall and carried himself well for somebody in his eighties. He was very suntanned and there was not an inch of fat on him. Julie got her blonde hair from her mother, Maureen, a diminutive figure but with strong features.

'Sit down, you've some explaining to do.' Eric indicated a chair but there was no offer of tea or coffee and certainly no beer. Luke plunged right in, explaining about the Rent Party and the trip to Brighton. 'We did take precautions, except for one night. She assured me that she was OK just that once. Her periods were regular.'

'She certainly made a mistake there,' interjected Eric angrily.

Luke went on to explain about the cigarette packet, how he had gone to Woolgoolga to find out about Julie and the chance discovery of the cricket photo. 'Until two days ago, I had no idea of Julie's surname or the fact that I was a father. Where is Julie and where is my child?'

'Julie is about eight miles from here in the local cemetery. She died in a car accident. Carrie, her daughter, well, God alone knows where she is. Nobody in the family has seen her in nearly twenty years,' explained Eric.

The rest of the story came pouring out with both parents interjecting and commenting. Julie had decided on this overseas trip after dropping out of uni. She came back in a total whirl. She found it difficult to settle. 'I knew that there was something wrong,' said Maureen. 'Three months later, she broke it to us that she was pregnant.'

'We tried to do what we could but – in the end – it was agreed that she would go off to Woolgoolga and have the baby there,' commented Eric. 'Some years later, she got married to Ritchie, a right bastard if ever there was one. His only attraction was that he was into horses and ran a riding school. But they fought like cat and dog. Ritchie could not cope with Carrie, who was as headstrong as her mother. He drank a lot and sometimes beat Julie up.' Maureen began to sob quietly.

'Anyway, a way back, they were at a party. They had yet another row. Julie drove off; she was way over the limit. About fifty miles from here a dingo dashed out into the road. She lost control of the car; it rolled and caught fire. Luckily, nobody else was involved but a dog on another property heard the noise and kept barking,' Eric continued.

'And Carrie? Where's she?' asked Luke.

'After her mother's death, things got even worse with Ritchie. Carrie took off and said that she did not want to see any of us again. She was going to change her name and wanted nothing to do with anybody. We keep hoping that she will change her mind but no luck. We miss her,' sobbed Maureen.

It had been a three days roller coaster of emotion and suddenly Luke could stand it no longer. His body began to shudder, and tears rolled down his cheeks.

'You better stay the night,' said Eric in a conciliatory fashion.

Wednesday, 24th September 2008

The conversation was only slightly less stilted next morning at breakfast. Luke felt like a messenger bringing bad news in a classical play. His presence was a reminder of sorrow of which he was the unwitting cause. They talked in a desultory way of farming, which was in a bad way at the time. The property had been in the family for three generations. 'Only one out of three sons were really interested,' both parents agreed. The father marked Luke's map as to where the church grave yard was and where the accident had taken place.

'Promise me that if Carrie ever gets in touch, you will let me know?' asked Luke.

'Don't hold out much hope,' commented Maureen. 'That one seems to be gone forever.'

'If you want to know more about Julie', said Eric, 'you should ring Susie, her sister in Brisbane.' Luke knew that further discussion would only hurt them more.

He found the church without any problems. Luke always found colonial churches difficult to approach; the notion of an *ancient* building being nearly a hundred years old was slightly bizarre in the context of Britain. The church was wooden with a brick extension. He found Julie's grave without much difficulty. He wondered what to do and finally decided by taking a post card of Woolgoolga and writing on the back:

Death be not proud, though some have called thee
Mighty and dreadful, for thou are not so,
For, those, who thou think'st, thou does overthrow
Die not, poor death'

Donne's words were great poetry thought Luke but he found it difficult to cope with the notion of the afterlife. He placed it next to the headstone.

The scene of the road crash was more difficult to discover. He was roughly there but there was no precise spot to find. He stopped by the wayside and tried to find some trace but no luck. A truck drove up and stopped.

'Missing something, mate?' Luke explained that he was a friend of Julie's and he was trying to find the exact spot of the accident. 'I can help you there. I was the first there after it happened. Jim's the name, live over there. My dog would not stop barking.'

They walked about 50 yards and Jim pointed to a pile of stones. 'I put these there to mark the spot.' Luke could see that the stones at the bottom still had traces of burning. He put another stone on the pile. 'It's just one of those things that us blokes can't understand. Why do really nice Sheilas go off and shack up with total arseholes?' Luke could provide no satisfactory answer. They shook hands and parted.

A few miles down the road he stopped and called Susie, Julie's sister. A very crisp voice answered. 'Been expecting you to call. Come over and have a meal and stay the night. We have lots to talk about.'

CHAPTER NINE

BRISBANE

Wednesday, 24th September – Sunday, 28th September 2008

Luke could see why so many Americans felt at home in Australian cities and towns. Brisbane is very much based on a system of straight streets and blocks. Susie lived in a flat overlooking the river. She was about four inches shorter than Julie, much more like her mother; cropped blonde hair with a few streaks of grey, pale blue blouse, fresh laundered jeans and minimal make up. The flat was neat, functional and well organised with a few landscape paintings. Not a lady, Luke thought, who read poetry and rode horses.

A few glasses of wine loosened them up over a salad meal. 'Yes, she told me all about you when she got back,' explained Susie.

'How did she know my surname?' asked Luke.

'You had it in the front of the poetry book. That's how Julie was able to put your name on the birth certificate.' Boarding school training, thought Luke, anything that did not have a name in it was community property. He had forgotten all about that.

Susie, it turned out, was divorced and a chief accountant with a stockbroking company. Her main interest was sailing.

'Julie and I were very different but we were very close, especially when her marriage went wrong. She was a couple of years older than me, but we were the only two girls in the family, so we stuck together.'

Next morning at breakfast, she handed him three large cardboard boxes. 'Here's what Julie thought important. This is the stuff she kept. She left it here, as she didn't want Richie nosing around. Have a look while I go to work. You better have this back as well.' She handed him his book of poetry.

It took him all day to sort through the contents: school books, cuttings from magazines, rosettes from gymkhanas, pictures (mainly black and white) of holidays, old 45s, school life and groups of friends, and even the odd school report ('Julie needs to pay more respect to school rules' seemed a common verdict).

He found a copy of his first book, ordered from Folio Books of Albert Street. Thank goodness, he thought, that I kept my promise and dedicated it to her. Girls' belongings differed very much to boys, in many respects, but he smiled at a set of initials that he had not seen in over forty years. PRIF = PLEASE RETURNED IF FOUND.

With a degree of embarrassment, he read a brief diary kept when she was 13 years old. It was full of horses and a crush on a boy called Arnold.

That evening, he broached the subject of Carrie. 'It was a real mess. Ritchie could not really accept that the child was somebody else's, especially as they did not have any of their own. I often wondered how keen Julie was on that and whether she did anything to stop it happening. Carrie was even more wild than Julie and, as the rows between her and Ritchie got more bitter, so the youngster got more out of control. When Julie died, Carrie was distraught, and things got even worse. She used to come here sometimes with enormous bruises where Richie beat her. She left a letter after a year and said that she was changing her name and was not coming back.' Susie's voice faltered, as she tried to explain.

'Nobody has heard anything?' enquired Luke.

'Not a word.'

After dinner, Susie went to the bureau and got out a package. 'Here, you ought to look at these.' She handed him about 20 pictures of Carrie from babyhood to her early twenties. She had his dark hair and was tall, like both her parents. The smile was undoubtedly Julie's. Luke looked at every one for several minutes. 'My daughter,' he exclaimed,' my daughter.' He put his head in his hands and wept.

'Yes, there's no doubt that she's yours,' commented Susie with an arm around his shoulder in support.

He trudged around Brisbane next day in deep depression. The death of Julie had ended his dream of finding her, however unrealistic. The thought that he had a daughter hit him hard. He'd never had children, thanks to relationship breakdown and different priorities. Now, Carrie could be anywhere on the globe.

He plodded around the main tourist attractions: the Museum, the Cathedral and the Customs House. He took in virtually nothing. Not even finding out that there was a place called Vulture Street could raise his spirits. (Australia has a lot of deadly species but no vultures.) The Gabba cricket ground was too far out to walk to.

He pondered the future over a coffee in an Italian cafe. Nobody, apart from Henry, knew the real reason for him being in Australia. His house was let for six months. He had no reason for being back in Britain. He had what Jane Austen's generation would call 'sufficient funds'. The trouble was he had not the slightest idea what he would like to do, apart from finding Carrie. He smiled for the first time that day at the thought of what Lord Melbourne, the early 19th century Whig Prime Minister, might have done (a very appropriate reference point for Australia, as the name of the Victoria's state capital). His Lordship's response to many crises was to do very little or nothing at all. Events often either changed or went away; sometimes they simply sorted themselves out of their own accord. Luke wondered how he would cope with an in-your-face media and a universal franchise.

It was in the State Art Gallery that inspiration came. He gazed at some Aborigine art that was on display. He was too fatigued and depressed to take very much of it in, but did recognise its intensity and its totally different cultural focus and values. An idea began to develop, as he gazed at this completely different mindset.

A bizarre thought: Lord M meets Aborigine culture. He knew very little about Aborigines but he had heard of Walkabout. Instead of deciding on a plan, he would take life in the next few months as it came. He would have no objectives and no timetable. He would let life just happen. He realised that for Aborigines it an important spiritual dimension; perhaps that would be the same for him too?

He explained his idea that night in a low-key bistro round the corner from Susie's flat. One thing that Luke very much approved of was BYOG – Bring Your Own Grog. Many Australian restaurants, especially in the cheap and cheerful category, allowed you to bring your own wine or alcohol; a few of them charging corkage. Luke had often fumed in Britain, when eating out at being charged £15-20 for a bottle of wine, that he could pick up for £5-10 at a supermarket; the wine often costing more than the main course.

Over the light of a candle stuck into a bottle of Hardy's Red wine, he explained his ideas to Susie. 'For the first time in my life, I have no deadlines, no meetings to attend, no lectures to give and no schedule at all. I have enough money for a few essentials, and I would be happy to do casual work some place. I could even let my flat for another half year if I wanted to.'

'As a Queenslander, I disapprove instinctively of anything to do with Melbourne but it does seem a beaut idea. Here's to your Walkabout.' They clinked glasses and then started to make a list of things he need to do on the back of a paper napkin.

Luke's spirits lifted now he had a fixed plan. For the next two days he bought the essentials for his trip: *The Australian Road Atlas 2009* (already published), a sleeping bag, a tent, cutlery, a primus stove, Rough's *Guide to Australia,* and a very large water bottle. 'You have forgotten one thing,' commented Susie, as she contemplated the rising pile of equipment in her living room, 'an Esky.'

'What the hell is an Esky?'

'What you Poms would call a water cooler. You put ice in and it keeps the beer and wine cool.'

The most difficult decision was getting some wheels (Luke's knowledge of mechanics was non-existent). It was solved by a client of Susie's firm, who was a motor dealer. 'I recommended some shares to him that came good.' After a test drive round the block and a can of 4X beer each, they agreed a price on a 1984, Red Belmont Holden Ute. A ute, it was explained to him, was the ultimate Australian mechanical experience: a two-seater utility wagon with a large open back, often covered by a canvas sheet.

'She's got over 80,000 miles on the clock but she will do you for a year,' claimed the owner. And so, it proved.

That night they ate at Susie's. Over a roast chicken and a couple of bottles of wine, they got mildly drunk and reviewed their lives. Susie's divorce had been more a drifting apart. 'I never wanted children, too much a career girl.' There had been 'a couple of other blokes afterwards but nothing really serious.' Just before they piled into the cheese and some Bundaberg rum (inevitably known as a Bundy) – Susie went to her bureau. 'You need to see these'. She handed Luke some pictures of Julie, taken just before she died. 'Both of you idealised an image of each other, especially when things went wrong in your marriages.'

Luke gazed at them. They were Julie but a slightly different Julie. She had kept her figure but was maybe a quarter of a stone heavier. The hair was still blonde (with a little help?) and there were some lines under the eyes and a few wrinkles (no makeup?). The smile was the same. Luke thought, 'I could still get along with her.'

They piled the dishes on the side and had a nightcap of some more Bundy. Eventually, they stood up and embraced. 'Good luck, I hope you find what you are looking for.' Luke fell into a trance but at some time during the early hours, he felt someone slip in beside him and wrap herself around him. 'One for the road,' she whispered into his ear.

Next day, Luke awoke to an empty flat. 'Early start,' the note said, propped up against the toaster. 'Help yourself. Stay in touch.'

Luke piled his kit into the ute and drove to the end of the road. He stopped and tossed a coin. Tails – he headed south.

PART THREE

Walkabout

CHAPTER TEN

SNAPSHOTS

Monday, 29th September 2008 – Friday, 20th March 2009

'Walkabout refers to a rite of passage during which male Australian Aborigines would undergo a journey during adolescence and live in the wilderness for a period as long as six months... To Aboriginals, spiritual matters take priority over mundane routine. Walkabout is a time of reflection in solitude from community and mundane routine, a time to detach and fortify the spirit. White society, whose existence may be more mundane, fails to recognize and prioritize spiritual needs, and only partakes in walkabout when it is forced upon them in the form of depression and mental illness.'

Wikipedia

When he looked back at his time of Walkabout, Luke saw it, not as a continuous narrative, but more of a mosaic of jumbled snapshots.

Luke had started at the Great Barrier Reef. Few things in life are more reassuring than finding something as impressive as you imagined it. Like most tourists, he joined a day trip that took him out to the edge of the Reef and he was able to snorkel and see some memorable sights; large fish swam past him and he was even able to cling on to one. Shoals of smaller fish of all colours sauntered by him in a lazy mass. The coral in all shades were simply beautiful. The sea was deep blue with astounding clarity. However, he had a depressing conversation with one of the passengers, who turned out to be a geology professor from America. 'It's amazing but it is being eroded, despite the best efforts of the Aussies. Water pollution, climate change and coral bleaching means that this is a shrinking site,' he commented sadly.

The most bizarre incident occurred on the Indian Pacific railway from Perth to Adelaide. It included a 297-mile straight line of railway – the longest in the world. Luke thought of the early explorers, who had tried to cross the bleak, treeless waste land of the Nullabor Plain. The train stopped at several halts on the way. At Cook, a welcome sign read, 'If you're crook, Come to Cook.' A sign outside the local store read: 'Any Arsehole that steals from this camp will be gut shot and left for the eagles to feed on.'

In the middle of the desert, the train's axle broke, leaving it stranded. The passengers in the cheapest seats decided to throw a party, while waiting for the replacement train, as they looked out over some of the bleakest landscape on earth. As they chatted, drank wine and sang songs to a Canadian's guitar, Luke wondered what the explorer, Edward Eyre, who first crossed the Nullabor, would have made of it. Luckily, the air conditioning was not affected. Just as the party was reaching its climax, his mobile rang. It was his lodger from England. 'Can you explain the central heating?'

Luke's most depressing evening was on New Year's Eve (always a bad time for him) at a pub in Newcastle on the New South Wales coast. Two very drunk rival teams tried to outdo each other in making pyramids out of empty beer cans. Inevitably, there was much singing, some vomiting and throwing of missiles. The noise grew louder and the smell became overpowering. A fight broke out and the police arrived. Luke felt lonely and isolated.

His most confused time was in Darwin, where he attended a talk on a new programme for Aborigines. The speaker and his audience were obviously sincere and outlined new initiatives and ideas. Luke knew that in the last forty years or so, much had been done on land rights, political involvement, social equality programmes and health issues. The problem of racial harmony remained and was symbolised by the fact that there were only a handful of Aborigines in the audience. They seemed openly dismissive of what was being discussed and argued amongst themselves.

At the edge of many country towns were camps of Aborigines. They seemed to have lost some of their own culture and embraced all that was worst in European, especially over the use of drink and drugs. The number of Aborigines in Darwin in relation to whites was rising. Locked gates and guard dogs in middle class areas highlighted growing tensions. 'You don't make me equal by calling me a fucking First Australian,' spat out one of the few Aborigines at the talk.

For much of the time, Luke was alone with his thoughts. He remembered Pam, his first wife. It seemed that he was the last to know of the affair with somebody from her office. In retrospect, there were clues all over the place: long business week-end meetings; phone calls broken off; and a growing detachment. Ironically, things came to a head on Valentine's Day; over a glass of wine and by candle light, when she told him that she was leaving. She did not even stay for the dessert.

His second marriage was almost a classic university one. Wendy was a PhD student, whom he was supervising. She was in her late 20s and they seemed to slide into marriage. Tutorials started in pubs but switched to restaurants. Books he wanted to lend her were at his home. Discussion grew longer and more general. She started to stay the night and soon vacated the spare room. The PhD turned into a book and she was lucky enough to get a lectureship at another university. The 300-hundred-mile journey between the two of them just about worked for a bit but not for long. How much of this was his fault, he wondered? His decline in interest in his job: was it a symptom of his unhappiness or was it the other way round?

CHAPTER ELEVEN

BUSHFIRE

Saturday, 7th February 2009

Luke gazed at himself in the mirror during an early morning shave at a hotel in Melbourne. It was already hot, prickly heat hot. Australia was experiencing one of the worst heat waves in its history. He had been in Melbourne at the end of January, when the temperature had reached 113 degrees Fahrenheit (Luke still traditionally measured temperature). Everybody wanted shade, cool and air conditioning. As February started, the heat grew even more intense.

It was early morning and already in the 80s. Luke realised that he had not smoked for over a month, not through any conscious policy; he had just not got round to it. He was also half a stone lighter but was drinking more. He had drifted from contact to contact and from one situation to another. He had arrived, as a backup, with a list of addresses from friends, school and university. He soon realised that nearly everybody in Britain seemed to know somebody who would 'probably put you up if you were passing.' People had been very kind and had sent him onto other friends and relatives. He had chopped wood, babysat, done bar work in a golf club and delivered groceries. He had just come from a fortnight of grape picking in Mildura and was feeling pleased with himself. He had managed to keep up with a young crowd, mainly made up of backpackers on their gap year. They had nicknamed him 'uncle' and he was amused to find that a couple were going onto his old university in September.

By midday, the temperature was at a record-breaking level of 115 degrees Fahrenheit. Going outside was like being punched. Every surface was untouchable. The night before, the Victorian Premier, John Brumby, had warned what the next day could be, 'It's just as bad a day as you can imagine. On top of that the state is tinder dry. People need to exercise common sense tomorrow.' Next day was to prove him right. The wind rose to 60 mph at midday, bringing down power lines and the fire started around Maysville and Kilmore East.

Luke watched on television as acres of land were on fire. A dark blanket of smoke hung over the city and by night 14 people were dead in what was to be called Black Saturday. Several weeks later, the total of deaths had risen to 173 and over 3000 buildings had been destroyed. There were many scenes of wonderful bravery and terrible grief. As in most disasters, there were heroes and villains. Awful to think that some of the fires were started by arsonists and there were some cases of looting. He could now understand why a group of Australians had burst out laughing when they were all together in a British pub during the hot summer of 1976, watching the news. A group of Brits, with handkerchiefs on their heads knotted at each corner, were beating in a desultory fashion at a few flames in a field of gorse with some brooms. It looked so amateur, compared to the Aussie high-tech battle with miles of flame and smoke.

Luke felt the need to talk to somebody in this crisis. He had written to Henry and explained the situation. He had only minimal contact with Susie, just a couple of brief post cards. Her absence on his departure day indicated that she was not keen on any kind of relationship.

He turned down the sound of the reporting of the fires on the television and rang her. 'Thank God, it's you. Really important news, I have been hoping that you would get in touch. Ritchie is dead. '

'Why is that important?'

'He left no will. Carrie is legally adopted and should inherit the property but she can't be found. His family is very keen to take over. He died suddenly while chopping wood. You need to come back as soon as possible. We need to fight this for Carrie.'

CHAPTER TWELVE

PREPARING FOR BATTLE

Tuesday, 11th February, 2009 – Friday, 20th March 2009

It took three days of driving to get to Brisbane. Luke drove mainly at night to escape the heat, holing up in the air conditioning of motels during the day. He felt that he was in his own bubble with voices from the radio echoing through the dark.

Voices of extreme grief: 'It's been our home for forty years and now it is ashes.'

Voices of deep anger: 'If I could get my hands on the bastard that started this....'

Voices of emollient officialdom: 'Please can everybody stay calm in this most difficult time?'

Voices of deep core sadness: 'We have lost our only child and just don't want to go on.'

Voices of exhaustion: 'The fire fighters have been going 24/7. They are even falling asleep as they eat their food.'

He arrived in the early evening and Susie explained the situation to him. 'Ritchie's brother, Greg, and his family have moved in, making a big deal of the fact that there is stock to feed and crops to harvest (although whether there will be anything left after this drought is another matter). He's a bigger bastard than even Ritchie was and it will be a devil's own job to get him off the land, especially as nobody has seen head nor tail of Carrie in over twenty years.'

'What's the legal situation?'

'I've got an appointment with a lawyer tomorrow. You need to come along. By the way, you almost look Australian.'

'Is that a compliment?'

'You'll pass till you open your mouth.'

'God', thought Luke next day, 'lawyers are all the same.' They sat in a sleekly functional office. Across a large desk, covered in files, was a corpulent figure with a beer gut protruding from his trouser waistline. He spoke in the clipped legalese of lawyers the world over.

'This case is covered in Queensland by the Succession Act of 1981, section 35, the Distribution on Intestacy is determined with reference to Schedule 2 of the Act,' he stated.

'What does that mean in English?' asked Luke.

'If X – in this case, Ritchie – has no spouse or *defacto*, then X's issue is entitled to a whole of the estate. If a member of X's family or another person was a dependent of X, they may have a claim on the estate.'

'What happens if the person inheriting cannot be found?' demanded Susie.

'Then the next in line of X's family, for example, a brother or sister, may make application for letters of Administration, but will have to prove that all steps have been taken to locate the stepdaughter and must satisfy the Court that she cannot be found or is dead.'

'So, if we can find Carrie, then the estate is hers,' Luke interjected.

The lawyer closed the folder with an air of finality. 'She would be entitled to a Grant of Administration and be given the ownership of the estate in Queensland,' he agreed.

They discussed things over a Spaghetti Bolognaise and some red wine that night. 'You can bet your bottom dollar that Greg will be getting the same advice from his lawyer,' she commented, as she ladled out second helpings.

'We obviously need to find Carrie and quick,' said Luke. 'How long do you think we've got?'

'That's up to the court to decide but not that long. A Queensland judge would likely be sympathetic to the idea of not letting a property stay empty for long, especially as there is stock and crops. He is likely to give a time limit and allow Greg to stay there in the meantime.'

Luke set up an office in the spare bedroom. His window looked over the harbour and, on the desk, he placed manila folders. His blood was up. He had never had a daughter before and the very least he could do was to help her.

CHAPTER THIRTEEN

LET BATTLE COMMENCE

Sunday, 16th February – Friday, 20th March 2009

They soon settled into a quiet limbo of domesticity. Susie worked long hours and often brought work home. The phone and the internet had changed research. Luke thought of the hours of investigation that could now be done by a quick click on Enter. It did not take long to find that Carrie had applied for a passport in March 1987 and had flown out of Australia to London a week later. Then the trail went dead. There was no record in Britain of any marriage, children, residency or phone number. 'Not even Facebook,' thought Luke.

He also prepared for his return to Britain with long calls to his estate agent and solicitor. 'You have a pile of letters about a foot high,' the latter explained.

Luke watered the garden and attacked the weeds. He did most of the cooking and Susie did the washing and ironing. 'It was almost like marriage without any of the complications,' he mused. For the first time in his life, Luke was almost oblivious to what was going on around him. He watched virtually no television and bought no newspapers. On Sunday, 22nd February, Australia held a National Day of Mourning for those killed in the bushfires. Luke did something on that day, which he had not done for years; he went to church. In the confines of St John's Cathedral and its Gothic architecture, he prayed for success in his search. 'I know it's hypocritical and I don't know if you exist but help me in my quest for my daughter.' He put a $50 note into the collection as a good luck token.

Susie counted up every Friday all that they spent that week in a yellow notebook and halved it. Ever the accountant, she got it right within seconds to the last cent. They did not mention their one night of intimacy and hardly referred to Julie at all. They sometimes did not see each other for a couple of days, instead leaving notes for each other. There were, however, uncanny echoes of his chats with Julie when they both reviewed their lives thus far. Occasionally, they went to the cinema and the theatre. They liked *In Bruges* and hated *Three and Out*. Their one trip in her yacht was a total disaster. Luke was a hopeless crew member and they were laughing so much that they capsized the boat. 'Shit, that's the first time that has ever happened to me,' she complained, as they righted the boat.

'Are there any sharks around here? asked Luke.

'Too bloody right, plenty of bull sharks. Let's get out of here,' declared an anxious Susie.

On the night before he flew home, they ate a BBQ meal on the veranda. Below lay the boats in the harbour and the sea gulls flew overhead calling out.

'Here's to your search,' she raised her glass.

'Amen to that,' he replied. 'But I've got something to confess. I am not only looking for Carrie. As I have driven around Australia, I have become more and more determined to find out who exactly I am. Who were my parents and why was I adopted? I want to know where I came from. I won't rest till I find my daughter and find out who I really am.'

'Good luck,' she commented. 'But be careful, as you have already found out, research can result in some unexpected consequences.'

'I know but I have got to find out. The need to know has grown stronger in me every day.'

PART FOUR

Dead End?

CHAPTER FOURTEEN

'THE LADY SEEMS TO HAVE VANISHED WITHOUT TRACE'

March – April 2009

'Anybody who has been at boarding school will know the depression of Sunday afternoons,' thought Luke. His return to England seemed initially to be one long Sunday afternoon; overcast day followed overcast day, interspersed with some drizzle and an occasional burst of sunlight. The spring weather matched his mood, as he attacked piles of correspondence and sorted through the dross of dealing with his return. Luckily, his tenants had kept his house in reasonable condition and had even left a nice note and a bottle of wine.

His search for Carrie did not get any further. In desperation, he sought professional help through an agency but with no luck. 'The lady seems to have vanished without trace,' said the owner as he placed a generous cheque in his wallet after a week of fruitless search.

He produced a large folder, which duplicated much of what Luke had already discovered: no traces in voting lists, telephone directories or travel details. There was no luck with mobile phone ownership or social media. The internet produced many Carries in most continents, but none could possibly be her, especially the Canadian glamour model, who seemed to spend a lot of her time posing nude or semi-nude for garage calendars.

Luke's depression was heightened further by an email from Susie. 'Court has given Greg six months and then a final decision will be made. His family are based there and are looking after the property. Unless you can find Carrie, the place is going to be his.'

Luke decided to start a quest for his own background. He eventually located his birth certificate and really gazed at it for the first time. His parents had filled out the forms for his first passport when he went on a school trip. Until then, he had travelled on his parents' passport. He found it difficult to take in what he saw. Father's Name: Unknown. Mother's Name: Unknown.

Luke was a foundling.

CHAPTER FIFTEEN

MEMORY BOX

Friday, 3rd April 2009

John Melville and Son is a firm of solicitors of three generations standing. Their Georgian office looks down on the square of the nearby market town. Luke's parents, grandparents, cousins and other relatives had their affairs sorted and advised, while ensconced in the firm's comfortable leather armchairs.

'Did you know about this?' asked Luke of the senior partner, showing him the birth- certificate.

'Yes,' he replied, 'I know all about it. Your mother discussed it with me several times after your father died.' Now in his 70s but still regularly attending the office, he looked the kind of man, who used to dispense wisdom while smoking a pipe. However, Luke noticed a discreet 'No Smoking' sign in the corner. He could do with a cigarette himself; he had fallen from grace since being back in England.

'Your mother was very keen that you should be fully briefed, but only if you showed any interest in your background. The family never hid from you that you were adopted but you did not seem to want to know any more. She was concerned that you would become upset and anxious, especially if you couldn't find anybody.'

He turned to a cupboard and removed a brown carboard container. On the front, Luke could see in his mother's neat writing: 'Luke's Memory Box.'

'Dearest Luke,' wrote his mother in the accompanying letter. 'I have thought long and hard about this and I hope that I have done the right thing for your happiness. We never had any children of our own (I had two miscarriages) and your adoption was such a blessing. Finding out that you are adopted is one thing but discovering your parents can be a very mixed blessing. I have read a lot about it and done some research. At best, it can be a joyful reunion. At worst, it can be a stirring of very unsettling memories for the mother and, sometimes, anger from the child at being given away. This is particularly true when there are no known parents. As ever, my thoughts are for your happiness and wellbeing. If you ever come to read this, I want you to know how proud of you, we both were, and no child was ever more loved. Your very loving Mother.'

The solicitor paused to let Luke take this all in. 'I know your mother thought a lot about this.' He produced from the box a Royal Stewart shawl and some cuttings from the two London evening papers of the time: the *Evening Standard* and the *Evening News*. 'Baby found at telephone box at the entrance to the park at Russell Square,' announced both papers. They described how a two-to-three-day old baby had been found in a portable carrycot by a postman, on his way to emptying a nearby pillar box.

'You were adopted by Barnardo's, after being taken into care,' continued the solicitor. The finder was Luke Clarkson; 'so that's how I got my first name,' thought Luke. He could not look at any more. His eyes were full of tears and he could not see properly.

'I suggest you take this away and look at it in your own time. It must come as a big surprise for you. The law has changed over recent years, and it is now much easier for adopted babies to find out about their real parents. But in your case, it is going to be more complicated. If you want, I suggest you contact the adoption agency.' The solicitor handed over the box and shook hands. 'Good luck! Let me know if I can help any further.'

A few hours later, Luke sat down with the contents of the Memory Box spread out on his kitchen table. There was a whisky in his hand and a cigarette waiting to be lit. The Royal Stewart tartan shawl was still in good condition and looked newly bought; so were the baby clothes and a light blanket. There were newspaper cuttings, not only from the London evening papers, but also from the *Daily Express* and the *Daily Mail.* They told in graphic detail of the discovery of the baby at about 6pm on the 21st July 1947. 'I heard a cry and swung open the door and there he was,' said his rescuer. A later picture showed him clutching Luke in an appeal to witnesses. 'He's a lovely baby. I can't see how anybody could leave him.' There were police notices, appealing for witnesses. More emotive still was a teddy bear with a bib, entitled Luke – a present from the nurses of the maternity ward of Charing Cross Hospital, where he spent his first few months.

Monday, 6th April 2009

Luke tried to follow his advice to his students when doing research. 'Always do the background first or you will miss a lot.'

He stepped out of Russell Square Tube station on a mild spring morning; daffodils were being sold by the entrance. Newspaper billboards were telling of an earthquake in Italy with many dead. As a postgraduate student, Luke usually got out at Holborn but, very occasionally, he would leave one stop earlier. He had enjoyed some lunchtime sandwiches in Russell Square during the summer; little knowing that this was the site of the discovery of himself as a baby. The ultra–Gothic Russell Hotel, which overlooked the Square, was a building that you either loved or loathed. Luke was a fan and had even occasionally drunk at the bar. The three red phone booths were still there by the entrance, as described in newspaper accounts of his discovery.

A few warmly clad couples were taking an early lunch and chatting over coffee or a glass of wine. There were banks of daffodils and splashes of crocuses and snowdrops.

Luke could not help himself. 'Please can you take a picture of me?' he asked a young woman pushing a pram. There were two phone booths next to each other and a gap of about six yards between them and the one where he had been found nearest to the entrance. Luke was pleased that the booths were still of the iconic traditional design, rather than the modern glass ones; exhibits of an age before the advent of the mobile and mass telephone ownership.

He hesitated for a moment, then looked down at the back of the booth on the right; the exact spot where he was found. 'Lucky, he had a good pair of lungs, or I would have missed him,' explained Luke's rescuer. The telephone had changed, of course, but the kiosk seemed to be largely as it was when he was found.

'The baby was well looked after and wrapped up warmly, even though it was a sunny day,' the reports had said.

Luke tried to imagine his mother getting off at the Tube and crossing the road as he had done. He had a sudden stab of anguish; he had heard that mothers usually waited around to see if the baby had been discovered. How long had she waited? Did she read reports in the papers? Did she ever wonder what had happened to him? What had driven her to this extreme decision? He tried to imagine the roller coaster of her emotions but failed. He looked at the park benches and tried to imagine where she might have sat. Not too near, in case somebody made a connection, but close enough to follow what took place. He picked a possible site, now occupied by an old man selecting some racing tips from the *Daily Mirror.*

Luke looked around the phone box. There was the usual juvenile graffiti, much of which seemed to feature Gwen and David. There were several cards for call girls, especially for Mandy, who was displaying a large amount of cleavage.

Luke began to cry again and then to sob.

There was a banging on the door. 'Have you finished in there, mate?' asked an exasperated voice.

Luke emerged into the pale sunlight. 'Yes,' he said, I've seen all I need to.'

It was only a short walk to the Foundling Museum at Brunswick Square. Luke had done some homework on its origins. The Foundling Hospital was founded in 1739 by Thomas Coram, a philanthropic sea captain. The lack of contraceptives, poverty and the stigma of illegitimacy, coupled with the traditional double standard, meant that London, like other urban areas, had masses of abandoned babies. In the period, 1756-1760 alone, 14,934 children were admitted, of which only 4,400 survived. A basket was left outside in which foundlings could be placed. If, to modern eyes, some of the practices involved were authoritarian, it was a brave and noble effort, which managed to gain not only royal and aristocratic support but also support from artists and musicians, such as Hogarth and Handel.

But the focus of Luke's visit was on the Tokens. When children were handed in, a note was made of 'any particular writing, or other distinguishing mark or token,' which might later be used to identify a child if it was reclaimed, explained the museum's guidebook. These were attached to a bit of clothing from the child. This was an age of mass illiteracy, but in many cases, great efforts had been made to make the Token recognisable by marks, initials or a few words, often misspelt.

It was the ordinariness of so many of the Tokens that Luke found so moving: buttons, keys, bits of string, ribbons, hairpins and all kinds of cloth and fabric. Some were more unusual: a diminutive bone fish, a hazelnut or a ticket to a philosophical lecture. One was rather ghoulish: 'Child 5588, John, renamed Robin Carr' was admitted with a caul, a piece of membrane that can cover a newborn's head and face. If the mother returned, she could reclaim the child, if she could prove that the child was hers.

The dedications were numbingly poignant. 'You have my heart. Tho wee muste part. I.W. 6 Sep 1759.' One disc had been taken from a beer bottle, labelled ALE. Harriet Woodall came to the Hospital in 1752 with a Token of a ring fitted with a small ruby and diamond gems and fastened to a small lock and key. It was accompanied by a ribbon rose and with an extract from the 23rd Psalm. The ring itself was engraved with the saying, 'Qui me negliege me perd.' ('Take care of me or you will lose me.')

A Charles II shilling was inscribed, 'Innocency in Safety.' The parents' initials were on the other side, RL and ED. The foundling was later claimed by his father, Richard Luke, in 1763 because he could accurately describe the Token.

A more tragic case was highlighted by a letter in 1757. 'Dear Sir, I am the unfortunate woman that lies under sentens of Death in Newgatt.' This was written by Margaret Larney, hoping that her children, who had been admitted to the hospital separately, might 'know one another.'

Unfortunately, the youngest child died shortly afterwards but the older child, renamed George Millet, thrived and became an apprentice to a wigmaker in Shropshire. Margaret was taken to Tyburn on a hurdle and executed by burning. Research suggested that she was wrongfully accused of making false coinage.

Mary Morris, mother of 'Charlot, renamed Barbara Turner,' returned several years later with a carefully preserved copy of the letter she had left with her baby, only to find that her daughter had died shortly after admission.

Luke walked slowly back to the Russell Square Tube, glanced again at that phone box and was unable to concentrate on the newspaper crossword on the way home.

Wednesday, 8th April 2009

It was not difficult to find Luke Clarkson. He had spent his life in the Post Office, working for over twenty years as a postie and then as a superintendent. He had also been active in the Union.

One knock on the door of a modest semi-detached in Acton and it was flung wide-open. Luke found himself in a crushingly warm embrace. 'Welcome. I have so often wondered what happened to you and I love the fact that they called you Luke. I last saw you when you were only a few days old.'

Over tea and biscuits, his rescuer retold the events of Luke's discovery. 'I was a little behind on the schedule and it was a sweltering hot day. Luckily, the traffic was not too bad, or I could have missed you. It's the only time in my life when I have dialled 999.

'I visited you once in hospital and I did think of putting in for adopting you, but the wife was not too keen. We were still hoping for some of our own but it never happened.

I wish Elsie, my wife, was here to see you but she died a couple of years ago.' Luke noticed a framed photograph of him as a postman in full uniform on prominent display on the mantlepiece. He thought also of how arbitrary adoption could be. He might have been raised in urban Acton, rather than in a large country cottage and garden.

'You must stay the night and there's a whole lot of people down the pub, who are dying to see you. They have heard all about you.'

It was a lovely night; the best since Luke's return and he found his general morale rising. 'I am dead chuffed that you have got my first name,' said his finder. As a student, Luke had done a couple of Christmas holiday jobs, delivering the post; so, he fitted in easily with the crowd that was mainly made up of working or retired postman. They were soon swapping stories of strange deliveries, aggressive dogs and weird English naming and numbering of streets. Endless photographs were taken, toasts made and rounds bought.

Near midnight, they made a slightly unsteady return to the house. Next morning, nursing a mild hangover, Luke was treated to a full works English fry up. On leaving, they embraced again. 'I'm so glad that it has turned out so right for you.'

Tuesday, 14th April 2009

'It's so much easier to find out about the details nowadays,' said the Clerk at the adoption society. He was in his 30s with ironed jeans and slightly long hair. 'Call me, Alec,' he said. He produced a yellow box file.

'Yes, there's only about 60 a year now in the whole of Britain these days with your background; more back then. Contraceptives on demand, abortion, morning after pills and changing attitudes to illegitimacy have changed all of that. Even my mum doesn't talk about 'living in sin anymore.'

Luke had spent an impatient few days waiting for this meeting but it was the Easter Bank Holiday weekend. 'I wish Christians would standardise the dates of Easter,' he thought, it would be so much easier for the rest of us. As he travelled on the Tube, he noticed that Phil Spector, the music producer, had been found guilty of murdering his girlfriend, Lana Clarkson. Ironically, after a few seconds he remembered that his finder was also called Clarkson.

'You can see here,' the Clerk continued, 'foundlings are put at the end of the list of births each month by the General Registry Office. Here you are registered at Bloomsbury.'

There were notes from the hospital. 'The baby is doing well and is putting on weight. The cutting of the umbilical cord seems a rather amateur job. The mother?' The Clerk pulled out notes from the police search. Posters had been displayed. A publicity campaign had been launched with a picture and story. A few letters and phone calls had been received but were obviously from cranks and those with a lot of spare time. How ironic, thought Luke, that half the world seems to want to get pregnant and the other trying to avoid it.

Luke smiled as he read his mother's application form for adoption; family administration was always her job. It would have been an ultra-critical social worker indeed, who could fault his parents as potential adopters. The report talked of 'reliability, financial security, stable home and a pleasant atmosphere.' Every box was ticked and a return visit to check on progress reported, 'Luke seems to have fallen on his feet.' The last document was a successful attempt to change his surname that of his adoptive parents. He was now truly one of the family.

Friday, 24th April – Sunday, 26th April 2009

Henry and Amelia had invited him for the weekend. 'We are dying to hear all about Australia and your adoption.' As Luke drank some excellent claret, he thought of the times when he and Henry, as students, had brewed beer in black plastic buckets. He expounded the details over the cheese at the end of a sumptuous dinner, served by Edith, the live-in cook.

'How keen are you *really* to find out your background?' demanded Amelia. 'Haven't you had enough emotional traumas for one life time?'

'My blood is up. I want to know where I came from. Also, Carrie is my number one priority. I think that somehow that both searches are linked together.'

Henry poured everybody another glass. 'It pays to advertise,' he said. 'I can get somebody from the office to do a media release. We will add some pictures and send it to all the papers. TV might also be interested. A double hunt for identity and whereabouts.' Luke realised that lawyers these days were very media savvy. He had seen Henry several times on TV, stating his client's point of view. He himself had done an interview on hospital radio and a couple on regional news for the BBC. However, he had never seen himself as a media don.

'You ought to get some secretarial assistance,' commented Amelia. 'You are likely to get a lot of replies, especially if you get on the telly. I am sure Henry's firm can provide you with somebody. You ought to find out about DNA. I was reading recently that estimates suggest that something like five percent of registered births have the wrong father on the certificate.'

There was one unexpected bonus to the weekend. Chris, the youngest child, had not followed in the wake of his very successful brother and sister and was finding teenage years awkward. 'I hate school, loathe games, don't want to do A Levels or go to university,' he confided to Luke over a pint at the pub, while they were meant to be going for a walk. Amelia pronounced his choice of career – 'mechanic' – with the disdain that would have done Wilde's Lady Bracknell proud. Luke, who had listened to a lot of teenage *angst* in his time, urged them to support the idea of an apprenticeship at a garage and one day a week at the local college.

'At least, it might cut down the garage bills,' grudgingly pronounced Henry.

When he got home on Sunday night, Luke rang Susie. 'I have missed you,' she said. 'It's dull here without you. I think you have got to do the publicity. You can't let Greg win.'

PART FIVE

Search Party

CHAPTER SIXTEEN

MEDIA LAUNCH

Thursday, 7th May 2009

Luke sipped a coffee in a meeting room at Henry's office. It was, he noticed, cafetiere not instant. It was accompanied by a plate of biscuits. 'Chocolate, one side; digestive the other,' explained the tea lady. He had difficulty opening the heavy drape curtains but discovered that it was done at the press of a button. When they opened, Luke saw all of Lincoln Inn Fields. He seemed to be the only male in the office, who was not wearing a tie. Luke was not entirely happy about the media launch.

'I don't see any other way,' emailed Susie from Brisbane. 'Greg is talking of planting for next year. There's only about three months left. I have enquired about an extension and the unofficial response is not positive. You have got to do this for Carrie.'

'If you are going to do this, you've got to go the whole hog,' underlined Henry. 'I think you will recognise one of the work experience people we have allocated to you.'

'Hello, Uncle Luke,' said a familiar voice. It was his godson, Arthur, Henry's and Amelia's eldest.

'For God's sake, drop the uncle,' replied Luke. 'It makes me feel a hundred.' Soon, Arthur was off to Harvard to gain international qualifications. He had – predictably – done well at Oxford, following in his parents' footsteps.

Amanda, the other helper, could not be more different. She was built like a prop forward and was clearly not a girl that was going to be put off by any public school-smoothie. 'Is that a Geordie accent?' enquired Luke.

'Sunderland born and bred. Mackem to the core,' came the quick response. Her ambition was family law. A good person to have on your side, thought Luke.

He was amazed by how professional the whole event was going to be. 'Putting your view out there, especially in civil cases, is really important now,' explained Henry. 'We are hoping to expand more into political and pressure group work. We are looking at this as some kind of training exercise.' Luke was shown the front cover of the launch folder with pictures of him with his finder and Carrie at 20. The assistants had assembled a whole range of other photos, including Julie and Carrie as a child. There were photos of Luke from student days to lecturer, photos of the phone box with and without his finder, Luke Clarkson, even a photo of the Royal Stewart shawl and the teddy bear with Luke on it from the hospital.

Luke Clarkson was thrilled to be included and stated that he 'would be delighted to pose for any photos.' Luke vetoed the idea of a picture of Julie's fatal car crash spot. A media release gave the basic details and some emotive quotes.

Amanda explained that Thursday was generally a good day for a media launch. 'You can get your story in the Sundays and 11am is ideal; good turnaround time for the dailies, the telly and radio. We think it could be big for the Women's weeklies, they should love it. Let's hope that there are no strong counter attractions.' Luke confirmed – with a few inner reservations – that he would be happy to do interviews. There was only one place the event could be held, the Russell Hotel, overlooking where he had been found. Tea, coffee and sandwiches were ordered. 'By midday, some of the hacks will certainly want a few beers or even a G and T or a Scotch,' predicted Amanda.

Arthur helped him with the DNA test. 'We have to do a few of these in paternity and divorce cases.' Luke spat into the provided plastic tube and Arthur sealed the envelope to get the results. 'It will take a few weeks but it could be a good follow-up.'

It was decided that Thursday 21st May would be launch day. 'Good luck,' emailed Susie.

Amelia announced that she was taking the day off to provide moral support; 'in any case, wouldn't miss this for the world.' When Luke suggested he pay for some of the event, he was told, 'don't worry, we can lose it in expenses.'

In the fortnight working up to the launch, Luke had plenty of time for reflection. Historians spend a lot of time debating the causation of events. Front runners include religion, predestination, Marxism and Feminism, to say nothing of the debate about nature/nurture. But Luke had often thought luck and chance had a very big say in the random nature of life; what Machiavelli called 'Fortuna.'

He agreed with Machiavelli that life seemed half determined choice and half chance. Here he was about to face the British media, as a result of events that started with a weekend some 40 years ago. He remembered a student, who delighted in quirky explanations, stating in an essay that the real cause of World War One was Frans Ferdinand's chauffeur, who not only took the wrong turning but also stalled the car opposite Gavrilo Princip. He couldn't miss, was the conclusion.

The same student argued that the cause of World War Two was Professor Wagner, the Head of Vienna's Art College (no relation of the composer), who turned down Adolph Hitler, not once but twice for admission. Luke had met his first wife, Wendy, on a train. If one or both had got into another carriage, they would never have met. 'For want of a nail, the shoe was lost,' claimed the proverb, showing how seemingly small events sometimes led to larger consequences.

Thursday, 21st May 2009

Luke was amazed at how many people turned up for the launch. The quest for a double search seemed to have caught the imagination. Arthur and Amanda gave out ID badges. Amelia supervised tea and coffee, while in the background, sandwiches and cake waited. The bar staff were on a midday alert. Luke felt slightly self-conscious in a suit and tie (his only concessions to dressing up were usually for weddings and funerals).

Henry introduced Luke – 'as a very old friend' – and then took the group through the media pack. Luke then fielded questions:

How did he feel now towards the mother that had left him? 'Love and compassion, for any woman deserting a few day-old baby must be heart-breaking.'

How did he feel about being a father? 'Wonderful, I long to meet up with Carrie.'

Why did Carrie leave home? 'The death of her mother upset her.' (Luke played down the inheritance aspect.)

Had he done a DNA test? 'Yes and, as soon as the results are known, they will be released.'

After the formal launch, Luke circulated the room, followed by Arthur and Amanda. On the spot interviews were conducted and appearances on local TV and radio were fixed. Two days later, he was to appear as a guest on Radio 2. There was an impressive turn out of journalists – broadsheets and tabloids. He posed for endless photos; some with Luke Clarkson, who lapped up the attention, fortified by several pints of beer. The women's weeklies were there in force; here was a story with a very strong feminine angle. Luke was pleased to see a solid turn out from Australia, led by the *Sydney Morning Herald* and the *Brisbane Courier Mail*.

Very soon, much of the audience spilt out across the road to the phone box for more photographs and interviews. By mid-afternoon, the crowd began to disperse, as journalists headed off to offices to meet deadlines. 'You did well, played a blinder,' commented Henry. Amelia, Arthur and Amanda were also enthusiastic. All that lecturing and giving tutorials must have been of some help, thought Luke.

A good luck email had come from Susie. That night, the support team headed out for an Indian curry. 'Here's to your real ID,' toasted Henry. In the morning, before the launch, Luke had surveyed the office, as they were all hoping for a good outcome.

Scrap books were ready, recording equipment stood by for TV and radio interviews and a filing system had been established. There were four sections – weird, personal (people relating to their own experiences), possible and, most exciting of all, probables. Luke waited with mounting anxiety to see what would turn up.

Friday 22nd May – Tuesday, 30th June 2009

Luke experienced every possible emotion in the weeks that followed. Every day, he trudged from Henry's flat, where he occupied the guest suite, to the office. Every morning, he reviewed progress with Arthur and Amanda. For the first time he realised the power of social media and it was not always a pleasant experience. His newly created Twitter account bulged with comment. He just about coped with being called a bastard and his mother, a whore. But the story unleashed a cesspit of abuse. There were an almost equal amount of messages of encouragement and best wishes. But Luke found the experience rather like Gresham's Law on fake currency; bad messages seemed to drive out good in the mind.

There were crank remarks, quoting the Old Testament, and ones that were simply dotty. A few, for some totally bizarre reason, linked the search to a Jewish conspiracy ('there's always a few that can slide that in anywhere,' explained Henry).

The coverage that the launch got was impressive. The world was trying to cope with recession and a flu epidemic but there were few competing personal stories. Chelsea won the FA Cup with a late goal and Man U won the League for the third time in a row. The cuttings and recording files began to bulge. Luke found some personal stories very moving and he was amazed to discover how many foundlings had been left in a bizarre range of places – railway carriages, lavatories, airport lounges and alleyways near pubs. There were even a couple of telephone boxes.

He was fascinated by the consequences of adoption and, in some cases, with meeting up with mothers some years later. Luke realised, yet again, how lucky he had been; as he read of cases of neglect, beatings and humiliation. Others echoed one respondent, who wrote, 'my step parents were wonderful examples of human kindness.' The success ratio of the meetings years later with mothers (and very occasionally, fathers) was about evens. Most had at least a degree of compassion but there were often feelings of abandonment. 'I was left like a parcel in a shopping mall at Christmas,' wrote one contact.

There were follow up stories with journalists, nearly all women, looking for a fresh angle. Luke even posed with a photo of Carrie and the Royal Stewart shawl in front of the telephone box. 'Try to look wistful,' demanded the photographer. Luke did more radio interviews; his knowledge of pop music had faded away somewhere in the mid-70s but DJs remained the same with forced good humour and talking too often through the start and endings of songs. He did not make a national television appearance but he did a London regional interview with the cameras following him across the park to the phone box.

One file remained depressingly empty. No mother stepped forward, not even crank ones. There were no sightings of Carrie.

'We are going to have to call it a day,' commented Henry at the end of June, 'I need to get Arthur and Amanda back to work.'

Luke returned home to a grey future.

PART SIX

Progress of a Kind

CHAPTER SEVENTEEN

RETIREMENT CAN BE TIRESOME

July-August 2009

Luke initially found retirement a very overrated business. He had lived in the same West Country village for over thirty years but had never really seen himself as a true local. He had drunk in the pub most weekends. He had an occasional meal from the visiting fish and chip van. He felt obliged to join the local history society but had found the standard of talks to be very variable; too many had wandered well over the hour and a half mark. He also found not all the topics, such as one on local ploughing competitions, to be of much interest. His social life had been mainly centred around the university, but now he found it difficult to pick up where he had left off. He had returned to the campus a few times but had found the students looking even more like children, though he fully realised that this was a product of his ageing. A colleague had explained his own retirement: 'when I started, I fancied some of the students, as I got older some of the mothers at graduation ceremonies were right crackers. Now, some of the grandmothers look all right.'

Luke made some half-hearted efforts at starting afresh. He shared an allotment for a short while but found that even his half share was too much produce for a single household. He found the politics of the allotments to be fiercely competitive and not just over whose sunflower or cabbage grew bigger. There seemed to be an underlying tension between the newcomer idealist, vegetarian/vegan group and the old sweats, whose patch had seemed to have been handed down since great-grandparents' digging had contributed to victory in World War Two. Battles and disputes were fought over encroaching boarders and occasional accusations of pilfering of produce.

Luke realised that his main (and only) hope rested with DNA profiling. Until recently, he had only been vaguely aware how much it had changed police work and researching into family history. It had been first developed by Sir Alec Jeffreys in 1984 and gained national recognition in the conviction of Colin Pitchfork in 1988 in the Enderby murder case. It was while watching Roger Federer beat Andy Roddick in the Wimbledon's Men's Final that Luke's DNA profile came through:

- England and Northwestern Europe – 23%
- Norway – 30%
- Scotland – 40%
- Germanic Europe – 5%
- Sweden – 2%

Even though it was an exciting match, Luke turned the tennis off and pondered the news. The English bit did not come as a surprise but 70% Scottish or Norwegian took some adjusting to. Visions of ancestors in kilts, wearing helmets with horns on them, yelling blood-curdling oaths and war cries, while involved in a ferocious battle, danced before his eyes.

Luke was excited and felt that at long last some clue to his identity had emerged. But he also realised that it had not taken him much further forward. A direct match could only be made through an analysis and link with a sample of blood, skin, saliva or hair; none of which existed in this case. A match could also be made if somebody else had made a voluntary check of their profile and it linked to Luke but DNA testing was still very much in its early stages. (He realised, with a wry smile, that of course he would not have access to police records.)

He was aware that family history was a boom industry with local county records offices full of researchers tracing their ancestors. (Many heartfelt thanks have often been said to the Mormon Church, which had pumped millions of dollars into family trees.) The Ancestry website was now in full swing and had been in operation since 1983. Luke felt that he had taken a step forward, but it was a very tentative one.

CHAPTER EIGHTEEN

A NEW RESEARCH ASSISTANT

Thursday, 20th August 2009

Luke had just completed a shopping list and was contemplating a visit to the supermarket, when some ferocious knocking nearly caused the door to come off its hinges.

Outside, stood Susie with two large suitcases, while a departing taxi disappeared around the corner.

'Good day! Do you want the Good News or the Bad News?' she demanded.

'The Bad News.'

'Greg has won; the property is his. He made a big thing about planning ahead with stock and crops. He used the failure of your publicity campaign to underline that Carrie had gone for ever and there was no chance of her reappearing.'

The news, delivered with typical Aussie directness, hit Luke very hard.

'And the Good News?' he asked.

'You have a new lodger and research assistant. I want to stay here for a while. We need to kick this thing on.'

They talked for most of the day and well into the night, fortified, inevitably, by another bottle of Hardys Red and the odd dash of Bundy rum. Susie would nod off for a short while due to jet lag but would then surface with renewed energy.

She commented: 'It's great news about a first step on the profiling, but who knows if it will take us any further. I love the idea of a Scottish and Norwegian background.

'I'm convinced that we can find Carrie. The more I think about it, the more I'm certain that she is not here in the UK. I think she almost immediately caught a ferry or plane to a European port. Who she met or what determined her plans, God alone only knows. The other thing is: I know Carrie! I think I may have an inside scoop into what was going on in her head.

'Since you left, her grandparents have been wracked with remorse and anxiety. They feel guilty that they did not do more to help, especially after Julie's death. We all do. Poor kid, an unknown farther and a witness to a toxic marriage.'

'Tell me, why didn't Julie contact me and let me know about Carrie?' asked Luke.

'She felt that you had both agreed not to see each other again. A parent that lived the other side of the world would not be much good. And then there was Ritchie.'

'What European countries might she have gone to?'

'It's only a guess but I would have bet on Greece, Spain or Italy. They're the mainland European countries that most Aussies would identify with. Melbourne has the third highest number of Greek speakers in the world after Athens and Thessaloniki. She didn't speak any of their languages, so she might have stuck out a bit to start with.'

It was nearly midnight and both were half asleep. 'There's one other reason that I'm here,' explained Susie. 'It's not often that I picked up on Julie's boyfriends, but you are a cut above the usual. We worked well together in Australia and I'm hoping that you won't make me pay rent but maybe we can split living expenses. I've retired from work and I'm looking for something to do.'

Luke guided her down the corridor and opened the door to the spare room. 'It's lovely to see you,' he said, 'we may be able to do great things.'

Sometime in the early hours, Luke's bedroom door opened. 'Move over' a voice said and its owner wrapped herself around him and fell dead asleep.

CHAPTER NINETEEN

THE ESSENCE OF GOOD RESEARCH IS ORGANISATION AND A DECENT FILING SYSTEM

August-October 2009

Luke and Susie largely slipped back into their life style they had in her flat in Brisbane. But it now felt much more than a professional search party. Realistically, Luke knew that this relationship could not be Julie Mark Two, but the more he got to know Susie, the more he got to like and, yes, increasingly, love her. What could easily have been a lot of mundane drudgery had an edge of fun and purpose. Susie's background in office management and accountancy was an excellent foundation for research. As Luke had told endless postgraduate students, 'The essence of good research is organisation and a decent filing system.'

They moved the large TV out of the sitting room and nicknamed it the Command HQ. At each was a desk overlooking the countryside. Four brand new filing cabinets were bought, after Luke's accountant assured him that he could claim for them as an income tax deductible. The dining room table was moved into the centre and converted into a work area. Over Luke's desk, he put three pictures: Julie, Cassie and his DNA profile. Before he put up Julie's photo, he very sensibly asked Susie if she minded. 'Not at all,' she said, 'after all, she was my sister and you didn't know me then.' Next day – without prompting – he added a fourth picture, taken of them together on their boat trip on Brisbane Harbour.

The hard facts of research had not changed. Airlines entering the UK only have to keep passenger lists for six years. Documentation of ship and ferry passengers were kept in the period 1878 – 1960 but have been discontinued. In the 1980s, immigration had been a very controversial issue in British politics, but it did not seem to include white Australians, who were in transit.

Susie designed a poster with a large picture of Carrie and a question mark. They added few a few lines of explanation, but they decided against a reward (although if something did come up, they agreed to acknowledge generously). They sent copies to the three most likely UK's European embassies and to their regional consulates. They also sent it to English language newspapers and magazines in those countries. 'Some expatriates make almost no effort to learn the local language, living in a largely self-isolating group,' explained the editor of a Spanish- based, English weekly.

'What makes you certain that she's not in Britain?' asked Luke.

'You forget that I have an advantage: I know Carrie! She was in a mood to do something rash. She wanted to kick over the traces. Like her mother, she was something of a risk-taker. Not many women would head to Brighton after a quarter of an hour's acquaintance.'

Luke enjoyed showing Susie the West Country and they made time for a few expeditions. Like most Australians, she had difficulty in adjusting to distances and time in rural England. Three out of the five roads in and out of the village were little more than cattle tracks with branches brushing both sides of the car: the driver rarely changing out of third gear. A trip to the Minack Theatre at the end of Cornwall to see a production of *Hamlet* was a great success. Susie loved the idea of a theatre hacked out of the cliffs, overlooking the Atlantic. A picture of its founder, Rowena Cade, sitting in a wheelbarrow, overlooking her work, was soon displayed on the mantlepiece. 'My kind of girl,' enthused Susie. A trip to the Eden Project was also a great success, although Luke's patience was tried by Susie reading every single word in the brochure and every line of posted information.

It was the Tarr Steps on Exmoor, however, which seemed to have the most lasting impact. They had come across them almost by chance when visiting Dulverton. Over 180 feet long with seventeen spans, it claimed to be the oldest surviving bridge in Britain, which was in constant use. Local legend dated it to prehistoric origins and the Bronze Age. Looking down at the worn stones with the river swirling below, they could both imagine the thousands of feet – human and animal – that had crossed before them. They relished local folklore, which claimed that the bridge was made by the Devil, as a place to sunbathe. For the first time in many years, Luke bought a poetry book, an anthology of love poems, and inscribed it for Susie.

CHAPTER TWENTY

CONTACT

Thursday, 1st October 2009

All relationships have an occasional downside, thought Luke, and Susie's unrelenting heartiness before breakfast was something of a downer. Luke's brain only really engaged after the second cup of coffee. (Susie had banned cigarettes.) That morning the duvet was flung off with a war whoop. 'There's a response on the DNA,' she shouted.

They stumbled, all arms and legs, to the laptop and there it was in the middle of the Ancestry website: ERIC FLETCHER, Uncle. This may be the most important thing I write, thought Luke, as he detailed his background on one side of A4. He was about to scan and send it, when he added, a last sentence, 'I can't tell you how important this is to me.'

They only had enough time to eat breakfast, when a reply came through. 'Urgent and important – come at once. Details too complicated. Can put you up.' There was an address of a farmhouse, a few miles from Kelso on the Scottish borders but no phone number.

'Do you want me to come?' asked Susie.

'Of course. We need to start packing.'

The nearest Luke had ever got to Scotland was a weekend History Conference, based at Durham University. There had been a spectacular Saturday evening reception sponsored by Jamieson whiskey. Next morning, partially as a penance for over-indulgence but also because he wanted to savour the internal grandeur of the solid Norman pillars and architecture, he attended early communion. Halfway through the service, he looked across the aisle and saw a monument to the founder of English history writing, a local boy made good, the Venerable Bede.

Susie drove most of the way. Like many Aussies, she found a gear stick, as opposed to an automatic, difficult to handle. There was an occasional expletive, as she forgot the clutch. They stopped only for fuel; Luke saw banner headlines of an earthquake in Sumatra with something like 3000 dead.

The Sat Nav took them through the Cheviots, everywhere there seemed a blanket of golden leaves. 'We don't have anything quite like this,' enthused Susie. It took them through a small village of a few hundred houses and a shop.

The farm house was imposing: white walled and three storied in about four acres; at the end of a mile long drive, surrounded by outhouses, a greenhouse, a large garage and a barn. At the start of the drive was a porter's lodge or granny annexe. Not much change out of a million quid here, thought Luke. They parked next to a dilapidated Land Rover, one of the old style with a split screen. Luke gave a large rap on the horse-headed knocker on the imposing front door. 'Best of luck,' he whispered and gave Susie's hand a squeeze.

PART SEVEN

Family

CHAPTER TWENTY-ONE

BRIEFING

Thursday, 1st October – Tuesday, 6th October 2009

'Come in,' said a voice with just a hint of a Scots accent. 'I'm Eric Fletcher and I used to live here. My eldest son, Roy, is in charge now. Don't worry, we have the place to ourselves for the night. The family is all off staying with Jamie, my other son. He farms down the road.' He led Luke and Susie down a woodened panelled corridor with hunting prints on both walls and a prominent barometer. A modernising hand had been involved in the kitchen, there was a lot of glass and new equipment, lighting everywhere, a large breakfast table but also a small tabletop for snacking and grazing. There was ample evidence of family occupation everywhere: pictures on a large fridge door; a notice board with all kinds of reminders and children's drawings; and a shelf of cook books. There was a well-worn dog basket and a cat flap. Eric turned off the television news.

He was a tall man, just over six feet, with slate grey hair, a blue shirt, faded jeans with toes pointing out from his sandals. Luke instinctively liked him.

'Would you like a cup of tea or perhaps, given the circumstances, something a little stronger?'

Luke took a gulp of whisky and began to explain his mission. 'I'm not here for any inheritance and I don't want to cause any embarrassment. I have known all my life that I was adopted but only recently did I find out that I am a foundling, left in a telephone kiosk. Until the DNA match, I had no idea of a Scottish connection.'

'Since retiring from farming,' explained Eric, 'I've become the family historian. It seemed natural for a farmer, who has always been involved in looking at pedigrees. I have collected photos, records, letters, wills and the odd press cutting. I'm amazed at what you can find on the internet. We have been here for about 250 years and at the moment the future seems secure. God alone knows what this EU will mean long-term.

'It's a mixed farm; we have about 1000 acres. At the moment, we are doing a lot of dairy, but the secret of success has been hard work and adapting to the times.' He smiled and took a large sip of whisky 'It's a fairly straight forward history with no black sheep, or, rather not up till now.

'There were three of us. My elder brother, Dick, joined the Seaforth Highlanders and died in France in 1944. Before Dick died, I was destined for medicine and university in Edinburgh. My guess is that you are somehow connected to my sister, Sheila. By the look of you, you are definitely a Fletcher.' Susie nodded. 'There are Fletchers, arrow makers, all over Scotland but you are from these parts.

'We were all brought up very strictly. We couldn't even do washing on a Sunday. Prayers before meals; two church services on a Sunday. My grandfather forbade newspapers on the Sabbath and the only books you could read, apart from the Bible, were *The Pilgrim's Progress* and *Foxe's Book of Martyrs*. Don't worry, we are a little more laid back these days.

'Sheila married the local doctor and had three children. She was a pillar of the community and now lives in the gate lodge. Her husband died a few years back.

'In 1947, she was away in London, learning languages and secretarial skills. I think this is where you may fit in. I propose chatting to her in the morning and I'm sure she will want to meet you. There is one thing that it's important that you should know. She is a very sick woman – cancer, I'm afraid – and the doctors don't give her much longer – a few months at most. She's well cared for and not in much pain.'

'When you see her, please give her this.' Luke handed over the Royal Stewart shawl that he had been found wrapped in. Eric showed them to a bedroom at the top of the main stairs, which was dominated by a grandfather clock.

'Make yourselves at home. I'm afraid you will have to grab your own breakfast and I'll join you when I have some news, when I have seen Sheila,' remarked Eric.

'You could play tennis in here,' commented Susie, as she gazed at the vast bedroom. A predictable row of pictures of both game birds and stag heads lined the walls. Everything seemed to be on a large scale, including a massive cupboard that lined one wall. The double bed underlined the impression that the Fletchers tended to be on the tall side.

Once again, Luke reflected on the chain of circumstances that had led him here. 'You're on your own tomorrow,' said Susie. 'This is one you have to face on you own without me'

Sleep did not come easily.

CHAPTER TWENTY-TWO

HELLO, MUM

Wednesday, 7th October 2009

Breakfast seemed to drag on endlessly. Cups of coffee were made but only half drunk. Luke and Susie glanced through old copies of *Country Life* and *The Field*, which were scattered about the sitting room. Yesterday's copy of *The Scotsman* had a feature on Lady Gaga and a Gay Pride March in Washington DC. Just after 11am, on the verge of making yet another coffee, Eric reappeared.

'Sorry to take so long,' he apologised. 'As you can imagine, your arrival has come as a total bombshell and was completely unexpected. There were a lot of tears. She desperately wants to see you but is very anxious that you will not be angry with her. I reassured her on that. The nurse usually brings her lunch and she then normally sleeps for some of the afternoon. Whether she will this afternoon is very doubtful. The family is returning later on. Can I suggest that you and Susie move into the gate lodge for a bit? The key thing is that you are a Fletcher and Sheila's son. Tomorrow, if you can stand it, I think you need to meet the rest of the family.'

Quarter of an hour later, Luke knocked on Sheila's bedroom door. There was a startled half cry. He had wondered what his first words would be. He moved forward a few paces to the edge of the bed, bent down, and embraced the frail body. 'Hello, Mum' was all he could mutter. Luke wrapped his arms around Sheila, as she trembled and sobbed. Her words were lost in the sobs. Through his own tears, Luke could about discern a very elderly lady with a blue shawl over her shoulders. She was propped up in bed with some pillows to receive her visitor with face powder and lipstick newly applied. She clutched the Royal Stewart shawl and Luke to her chest. They remained like that, locked in an emotional silence, for several minutes.

'Forgive me, forgive me,' she sobbed. 'There's never been a day, when I haven't thought about you. Eric tells me you have done well. Have you been happy?

'There's nothing to forgive.'

'Eric told me that you are called Luke. Can I call you that?'

'Only, if I can go on calling you Mum.'

When the nurse came with lunch half an hour later, she found them in an embrace with their arms around each other – still too overcome to speak.

By mid-afternoon, they had recovered enough to talk. Sheila's remarks were interspersed by sobs and tears. Occasionally, her body shook. Luke held her hand and now and then mopped her face with his handkerchief.

'It was all so different then. You've no idea of how things have changed. I was 18 and so innocent and naïve. Even things like periods were not really discussed or explained. I was sent to London to learn secretarial and social skills. That was the level of expectation for girls in those days. Halfway through the course, I found out that I was pregnant. It must have happened, when I was on holiday in Scotland in the autumn.

'You cannot believe the shock and scandal that this would have caused around here. Sex before marriage was sinful.

Bastards were condemned out of hand. Abortion was illegal and out of the question. In my block of flats in South Ken were some medical students; they put me in touch with a newly qualified doctor, who said he would help, but warned me that this would be his first delivery. I gave him £100 – all my savings.

'Giving birth was a nightmare. It took nearly all day and the pain was dreadful. I remember newspapers spread everywhere, kettles of hot water and lots of blood.

'I kept you for three days. You were such a sweet baby. I took a taxi to Russell Square. I thought that there would be a lot of people there, so you would be found quickly. Nobody would be paying much attention to me. Luckily, there were no street cameras in those days. It was late afternoon and I put you in the telephone kiosk, near where I was sitting, so I could check somebody would find you. It only took ten minutes. I saw the postman find you and he rang 999. Then I slid away, so nobody could trace me.

'When I got back to my flat, my blouse was wet with milk. That went on for a couple of weeks. I cried for days, non-stop. I went back to Scotland a few weeks later and shortly afterwards became engaged but I have never forgotten you.'

Sheila looked up and smiled. From out of the back of her much-thumbed Bible, she produced a blonde curl. 'I cut this from your head, the morning I gave you away.'

She nodded off again for a while but woke for some tea and cake. There was a pause in the conversation. 'I've got to ask you an important question,' said Luke. 'Who is my father?'

'He was the local Minister, Hamish MacInnes. He took advantage of me – I hardly knew what was going on – at the end of a choir outing. If I had revealed this, my family and his would be ruined. He was a good man – for all his faults

– and well-liked. That's probably where you get your brains from. He never tried it again.'

Her concentration began to waver. She ate hardly any supper. By early evening, she was asleep.

Eric helped Luke and Susie to move their few belongings to a spare room in the gate lodge. Things were explained to Shona, the nurse. 'It will be all over village by tomorrow afternoon.' commented Eric, 'She's a lovely lady but a great gossip.'

Luke looked in on Sheila one more time before going to bed. She had a slight smile on her face and there was a wisp of hair across her eyes. The Royal Stewart shawl was still clasped to her chest.

'There's no way round it.' said Eric, 'it's in at the deep end tomorrow. Meet the family for a drink. Shona is going to tell the village, so best to break it to the family as soon as possible.'

Thursday, 8th October 2009

Meeting the family went far better than Luke expected. He shook hands with all the men and social kissed the cheeks of all the women. Children ran in and out of the downstairs rooms; often followed by a menagerie of dogs of all shapes and sizes. Luke was saved endless explanations by Eric, who clapped his hands and, in the ensuing silence, explaining the background of the new arrival in their midst. 'You've only got to look at him to know that there is Fletcher blood in him.'

Before the festivities started, Eric had also tactfully organised a private meeting with Luke's half brothers and sister. Callum was a teacher at the local high school and Mike ran a garage specialising in repairing old cars. Sophie was a mother of three and ran her own business, she gave him a big hug. 'I always wanted another brother.'

Luke and Susie stayed three more days at the gate lodge. Sometimes, the conversations were prolonged and emotional. At other times, they said very little but just sat holding hands. Susie won great praise for picking a bouquet, which was placed on the small table by Sheila's bed.

With much effort, Sheila delivered an important message. 'I've only a short while left. I want you to be one of the pallbearers at the funeral. I have told the others and they agreed. I want the Royal Stuart shawl to be put in the coffin with me. Do you promise?'

'Of course, I do. I will make sure that it is done.'

Wednesday, 14th October 2009

On their last day, Eric held a small family lunch party. 'Everything we eat has been produced here on the farm,' he proudly proclaimed. 'Even the whisky was distilled only a mile down the road.'

Relief engulfed Luke. His research indicated that the chances of a successful reunion seemed to be about fifty/fifty. 'The flipped coin has definitely landed the right say,' he thought.

He bonded easily with Callum, who taught English. They were soon exchanging grumbles about exams and overcrowded facilities. 'But I wouldn't want to do anything else, even though the authorities are eating into the only perk of the job – long holidays. Teenagers are real Marmite, but most of them turn out really great. Occasionally, I feel like drowning one or two but am always glad that it is illegal next day.' Like many Scots, Callum believed that the nation's education system was superior to England's. 'Historically, we value education more,' he stated firmly. Luke declined to engage with a smile.

Mike was a little slower to unbend. Luke explained his lack of mechanical ability but they began to exchange stories of old bangers in the early days, when the MOT was something of a formality, especially in the countryside. They all laughed at Luke's description of his first student car, in which rust had eaten most of the boot and back seat passengers tended to get wet feet if it rained. 'About the only thing mechanical that I am any good at is a push-start,' he confessed.

Sophy and Susie hit off from the start and were soon chatting non-stop and putting the world to rights over a shared love of red wine. As Susie had been raised on a farm, she soon fitted in. Again, Luke noticed that even this small social gathering included a horde of dogs of all sizes.

The family photo happened spontaneously without any planning. They all drifted up to the Lodge in a swirl of laughter. Somebody produced a camera and, they instinctively formed a group around Sheila's bed. They posed for a serious picture; 'one for the scrap book,' explained Eric, and another with everybody laughing and waving.

Luke and Susie headed south on a wave of contentment.

CHAPTER TWENTY-THREE

FLOWERS OF THE FOREST

Friday, 29th November 2009

The phone call came about a month later. 'Eric here – Mum died in her sleep yesterday. The funeral is in three days' time. The whole family would like you to be there. They would like you to be one of the pall bearers, as she requested. No black ties or dresses please.'

'Of course, we will be there.' Boarding school had put Luke off ties for ever, but this was one occasion, when he delved into the back of the cupboard.

There could not be a more emotive setting, a grey brick church, dating back to the mid-19th Century. Around them expanses of heather and gorse with fields hacked out and marked by stonewalling.

They had arrived the night before and joined the family wake at the gate lodge. A few whiskies were consumed and some sandwiches. Luke was touched that Susie was also made welcome. The Royal Stewart shawl was still in place across Sheila's heart. Some prayers were said and some readings shared. Stories and memories dominated the conversation. As night came, the room was lit only by candles. Luke felt very much included in what was an emotional catching up session.

Next day, as the hearse drew up to the church, *Flowers of the Forest*, greeted them; its plaintive terms echoing around not only the church but the neighbourhood. The single piper, who played beautifully, was a slip of a girl from a neighbouring village. There can be few more moving laments. Luke knew that it dated back to the defeat of the Scottish army and the death of King James IV at the battle of Flodden in September 1513. The church was packed and many stood outside, listening to the service and watching on several screens.

Luke was petrified that he would drop his corner of the coffin but, luckily, found it easy to carry. The priest delivered an emotional eulogy, based on personal knowledge and acquaintance. He saw Sheila as part of the medical team, which was respected throughout the community. 'Those were the days when doctors sometimes drove to patients' homes, sometimes in the middle of the night.' He described Sheila as a mixture of a medical assistant, nurse, comforter and receptionist. 'Everybody knew that the door at the side of the house was never locked. She gave out medicines, tied up bandages and had a kind word for all.'

Ironically, Luke found himself next to a plaque, commemorating Hamish MacInnes, his father. He was praised as 'a good and decent man.' Luke was delighted by the choice of one of the hymns, *Glorious Things of Thee Are Spoken.* Then remembered that he had mentioned this hymn on his last visit. Even an agnostic, such as Luke, admired the forthright declaration, 'Saviour since of Zion's city, I through grace a member am. Let the world deride or pity, I will glory in thy name.' The congregation filed out to *Flowers of the Forest.*

What everybody called a repast or a purvey was held after the church service at the Fletcher home. Luke was amazed and impressed by the tact shown by everybody present; virtually all knew who he was and why he was there, yet no remarks or comments were made. Part of this was due to changing attitudes even in nonconformist Scotland. This was also due to the respect for the Fletcher family in the neighbourhood. But this was due mostly to the part Sheila had played in the lives of the community. Several women told him how she had helped them through childbirth classes and support. He was moved to learn that she had been at the birth for some single mothers and for those whose husbands or partners were away; the area had strong military connections. She had not forgotten the pain and fear of her first pregnancy in that small Kensington flat.

Nearly everybody told him, as they left, that Sheila had 'slipped awa.' Afterwards, he sat and looked over the farm and the surrounding area. His body shook and tears came in floods.

PART EIGHT

Carrie

CHAPTER TWENTY-FOUR

A KIND OF EQUILIBRIUM

November 2009 – August 2010

The next two years were ones of personal equilibrium. Luke's discovery of his background and the warm response he had received from his new family, provided a growing sense of inner calm; something he had not really achieved in any other part of his life. He was touched not only by Christmas cards from the Fletchers, but also by an occasional phone call (mainly about university entrance and writing UCAS references).

For the first time in several decades, he was again enthusiastically researching, writing and doing some occasional teaching. He enjoyed lecturing at the local branch of the University of the Third Age. He had been inspired by seeing a production of *The Recruiting Officer* by George Farquhar, written in 1706. He later discovered that it was the first play produced in the colony of New South Wales in 1789, involving convicts from the First Fleet. His interest was further increased by seeing a production of *Our Country's Good* by Timberlake Wertenbaker, based on these events. Luke was transfixed by the notion of art being performed in that very inhospitable climate and was soon planning a book about it. He was able to do much of the research via the internet.

But the bedrock of his contentment lay in the growing quiet intimacy of his relationship with Susie. There were a few disagreements but lots of good times. It amazed Luke that after only a few months in the village; she was on first name terms with virtually everybody. Even the post mistress, a bastion of the local Methodist Church and the cornerstone of village gossip, pronounced her 'a very nice lady' – the ultimate accolade. Amelia, after visiting one week-end with Henry, emailed Luke: 'Have known most/all of your girlfriends, mistresses and wives since you were 18. You would be crazy not to marry Susie. Thinking about cutting you off the Christmas card list, if you don't do the sensible thing.' Henry added, 'You know Amelia, as subtle as a punch in the mouth in a pub brawl. But I have to say, I agree with her.' A more unlikely endorsement came from Pam, Luke's first wife, 'You would be crazy to let her go. She's making you so obviously happy.'

Susie converted the garden from what Luke called 'an eco-dump' into a thriving patch. She relished the milder climate of England to grow plants and flowers that would not flourish in the Queensland bush. They shared the housework and Luke did the cooking; something that he had shown very little interest in before. He enjoyed showing her around Britain and the continent. Her enthusiasm and enjoyment gave him fresh zest and inspiration. They spent about eight months of the year in England and avoided winters by going back to Australia; they were lucky with some short term lets of their properties. Susie's parents were dead and her eldest brother, Roy, now ran the farm. They studiously ignored anything to do with Greg on Ritchie's former property.

But still nagging away was the whereabouts of Carrie.

CHAPTER TWENTY-FIVE

A CHANCE DISCOVERY

Wednesday, 25th November 2009

It was the Australian habit of shortening virtually every name that turned out to be the key. Reading the Sunday papers' supplements in the middle of the week, as was his habit, Luke saw an article in a travel section on the Greek island of Hydra. The writer trundled out every cliché about that part of the Mediterranean – 'enchanting…beautiful…and historic.' Luke's eyes skim read with only a modicum of interest. It extolled an island where there were no cars or motorbikes. It made much of the relationship between the singer Leonard Cohen, who lived on the island, 1960-1967, and Marianne Ihlen. (Luke loved Cohen's song, *So Long Marianne.*) The article also produced a long list of other artistic and literary celebrities, who had also lived there. Just as he turned the page, very much in browsing mode, he noticed amongst a long list of cafes and tavernas, the Welcome Fish Restaurant, run by Giorgos and his Australian wife, Caroline.

A sudden thought, Australians would abbreviate nearly any word they could. Could Caroline be Carrie? The article had a picture of the café, overlooking the harbour. Luke could not resist. He typed the name into the internet. Up came a whole lot of pictures, aimed at getting custom: many of the outside, singing and dancing, the menu, coming attractions and, then, staff. He called, excitedly, to Susie: 'Come quick.'

He began to scroll down. There were several of the owner (a fisherman, much was made of fresh fish), some waiters and musicians. Then, the owner's wife, Caroline.

'It's Carrie.' shrieked Susie. 'It's her, definitely.'

'What are we going to do?' demanded Luke.

'I think we should get in touch right away; no time like the present. The internet has got the address, phone number and email details. It's about lunch time in Greece, bound to be people there. I want to phone right now.'

She paused for a moment. 'Do you mind if I do this on my own? This is a complete shock.'

'Sure, I'll go for a walk. Good luck.'

When Luke returned half an hour later, he did not have to be a student of body language to know that the call had not gone well. Susie was in a state of complete shock; she had obviously been crying and her hands were shaking.

'It was a disaster. She doesn't want to see us or hear from us ever again. She slammed the phone down after only a few minutes and told me that she was busy with customers. She wouldn't explain but said she'd send an email in the next few days. Taking down my email address was about the only time that she was coherent.' Susie began to sob, 'she was so angry and upset.'

Friday, 27th November 2009

The text, when it arrived two days later, was stark and uncompromising.

'There is only one phone in the house and you rang at lunchtime, when I was serving customers. The whole place could hear every word. That is why I am writing this.

'Get this: I don't want to hear from either of you again – ever. Don't write, phone, email or, even worse, turn up. I am very happy here with Giorgos and our three children.

'Susie, our family was unloving and uncaring. You all knew that Mum and Ritchie had a toxic marriage. You have no idea what it is like to live in a house of tension and hostility. But it increasingly got worse than that. Do you know what it is like for a child to hear your stepfather beating your mother? Hearing the slaps, the cries and the screams? I used to hide under the bedclothes to try and blot out the noise.

'Why did you not do anything? I know Mum used to visit you in Brisbane but did you not notice when she came less often? The family hardly ever visited. None of you liked Ritchie but that was not enough. You didn't really do anything. Maybe Mum did not say enough. Three brothers and two grandparents did nothing. Do you wonder why I have had nothing to do with any of you since I ran away? Where was the support?

'After Mum's death, things got worse, far worse. Oh, I know you said the right things and I occasionally got invited out. But did you know that Ritchie was hitting on me? It built up in stages, each one worse than the last. I tried to lock my bedroom door but that meant that it just happened elsewhere. He got increasingly violent too. Sometimes, I had to wear a long sleeve blouse to hide the marks. And he would taunt me that I was only a stepdaughter, so that made it OK.

'Eventually, I did the only possible thing – I ran. I hitchhiked across Europe; got a ferry at Piraeus and it just so happened that it was sailing to Hydra. I got a job as a waitress and I ended up marrying the boss; a really nice and kind man. I know you have been looking for me; Giorgos' cousin is the island's head of police. But I've done nothing wrong; broken no law; and I am now a Greek national.

'And, as for you, my father. It's not nice being the product of teenage carelessness. How often, I heard my mother say it was the only time that she was not regular? You were also careless in leaving your name at the front of that book of poetry. So, you were on my birth certificate and a presence in the house. And because my mother was often unhappy, I think she often looked back at your short time together with rose-tinted glasses. Ritchie loathed your name and it came up in arguments the whole time. After Mum died, he used to taunt me with it. The final straw that made me run away was when he used it when he was trying to fuck my arse. I couldn't take any more.

'I realise that you have been trying to get hold of me, so I can inherit the property. I want nothing to do with it, even the name sickens me.

'Leave me alone and leave me in peace. Get on with your lives and let me live mine. I repeat – I do not want any further contact of any sort. Carrie'

CHAPTER TWENTY-SIX

MELTDOWN

December 2009 – January 2010

The email and its stark contents had a numbing impact and punctured all feeling of contentment. 'I feel so inadequate,' exclaimed Susie. 'I talked a lot to Julie, usually on the phone but she did visit occasionally. Queensland is not like Europe; most trips in the outback are hundreds of miles and can't be done in a day. I was involved in my own life; a career and divorce are big on time. As for Mum and Dad, and the boys; perhaps they should have done more? They didn't like Ritchie at all and Julie was kind of headstrong. They also did not like involving themselves in the running of another property, especially with a know all like Ritchie in charge. God, how I regret that we, and especially me, did not do more,' she sobbed.

Luke found it difficult to console Susie. Not only was she distraught but he found it impossible to accept Carrie's conditions. He was forever forbidden to meet his only daughter and his three grandchildren. As a symbol of his non-acceptance, he pinned up a picture of Carrie, looking friendly and welcoming in the café. She looked more like Julie, especially her smile, but she had his gestures; she could have been giving a lecture, rather than explaining the menu.

There was only one thing for it; his usual response to a crisis. After a couple of days, he rang Henry.

'Christ, you two can certainly drum up a crisis. I don't think you should try an immediate reply, however conciliatory. It was perhaps unfortunate that you put her on the spot in public.

'One thing that might help. Amelia and I are taking a second honeymoon in a month's time – now the kids are off our hands – to the nearby island of Poros. We could change our return plans and spend a few days in Hydra and do a quick check. Amelia would promise to be on best behaviour and we will on no account break cover.'

'That would be great,' enthused Luke, 'but do be careful. Try to take a few photos, especially of the grandchildren.'

Post card from Hydra, received in the New Year. 'They are a sweet family and the food is sublime. Success on pictures. We were slightly tempted to kidnap the grandchildren; they are so adorable. Full report when we get back. Love H and A.'

Wednesday, 6th January 2010

Luke and Susie barely allowed a few hours for Henry and Amelia to unpack before they were on the phone on a shared line. The call lasted most of the morning.

'We spent four days in Hydra and stayed in a lovely little hotel, right on the harbour, and we treated ourselves to a balcony. We ate lunch at the family fish restaurant and had our last night there as well; we even did some Greek dancing to a local band.

'We teamed up with an American couple. She is a doctor and he is a lawyer, so you can imagine we had lots to talk about! She is even more inquisitive than Amelia; so, we were able to get a lot of low-down.

'The essential thing is that Carrie is happy. She's gone completely local and is brown as a nut. She speaks Greek like a local and can even outswear them if necessary. The restaurant is very much her domain; she is the manager and they have a lot of entertainment in the evening, some traditional Greek and some more modern. Giorgos does some work in the cafe but is away a lot – fishing. The fish is delicious and we gorged ourselves.

'He is a sweetie, very in love with Carrie and a devoted father. She is a formidable figure: your brains and Julie's strength of character. When she waves her arms around; you can see that she's your daughter. Certain glances and gestures remind me of you. The kids, Dimitris, aged thirteen, Nicholas, ten, and five-year-old, Maria, are great. Thanks largely to the Americans, we were able to dig for some personal information. Carrie completely shut down on Australia. She never wants to go back or have anything to do with it. Vague outlines of family disputes were given but no real details.'

'Is there any way you can think of that we could see them?' asked Luke, 'I can't imagine never being able to play with my grandchildren.'

'If just one of us went, would that make any difference? She can't really blame Luke,' asked Susie.

'She never mentioned anything specifically about you Luke, but you are perceived as part of the whole package,' replied Henry. 'Carrie appeared very determined on no contact.'

'One thing that might help a little,' said Amelia. 'They are both on Facebook under their Greek names: helps them publicise the restaurant. We are now Friends. She does regular postings of the family and the business. You could link into our account and see some of the pictures. It would not be very much but it might be better than nothing.'

In a few days' time, a package of photos arrived. There were about 50; many of the grandchildren – playing, helping out, swimming, football matches and being with family and friends. Luke's favourite was of Maria, climbing the stairs to bed, clutching her favourite teddy bear. But there were also a lot of Carrie looking maternal: playing with the children; running in the parents' race at the local school; serving in the restaurant; and singing with a piano accompaniment. Luke and Susie noticed that in most of them, she looked happy.

January – April 2010

There was only one topic of conversation in the next few weeks. Luke could not accept that he would never be able to see his only child and three grandchildren. Susie was hurt and bewildered. 'Julie and I talked on the phone the whole time. I don't think Carrie realised how much. We were always very close. When Julie died, I did invite Carrie over but she often declined. Mum and Dad could have done more but I suppose that they belonged to a generation that believed in not interfering. We were also hundreds of miles apart; you just couldn't drop in.'

They discussed strategies endlessly. Some days, Luke believed they should just turn up. Other times, they both thought that a detailed letter of explanation would be the best way. Would a visit by one of them do the trick and, if so, who should go? How about an approach to Giorgos; would he be more understanding? Reports from Henry and Amelia suggested that in matters of the family, Carrie ruled the roost. They thought about an intermediary; somebody who could argue on their behalf. (Henry was an obvious candidate but he was already known to the couple.)

In the end, Luke spent several days composing a letter, pleading for a meeting and access. He underlined how much they wanted to support and help the family. Susie added and subtracted bits; it ended up as a joint endeavour. A fortnight later, a bulky letter arrived, carrying a Greek stamp.

Their letter had been unread and had been torn into pieces.

They became Facebook addicts. 'Worse than a teenager,' commented Susie. They obsessively watched over the next few months: the life and times of the restaurant (trade seemed good); Giorgos and his crew on his boat with a good catch of fish; and Carrie and her friends on a girls' night out. But it was the pictures of the grandchildren, which they pored over with compulsive interest: football matches; first day at school; birthday parties; and expeditions to the beach. The bright Mediterranean colours contrasted with the subdued shades of the English countryside.

April 2010 – August 2010

The news of Carrie pushed Luke and Susie further together but their relationship became more introverted. Discussion about Hydra was non-stop; over and over they rehearsed the options. When in Australia, they reviewed the situation with Ron, Susie's elder brother, who was now running the family property. 'I guess you can't force people to be friendly if they don't want to be,' he commented with a shrug.

Both felt aggrieved by the situation. Susie, because the more she thought about it, the more she felt that she had been misjudged, and Luke became more desolate, as he contemplated the future without seeing his daughter or grandchildren.

Facebook became even more of an obsession, especially when Carrie started to put up short videos. Like most amateur films, there were plenty of jerky, out of focus shots, which were often repetitive. But occasionally, with the luck of enthusiastic beginners, a sequence would be shown that would melt the heart and make separation even more difficult to bear.

In August 2010 the publication of Luke's book, *Raising the Curtain: The Start of Australian Drama* was a welcome distraction. It was published by his former university's press but unsurprisingly did not dent the figures of the best sellers of that year, *Jamie's 30 Minute Meals,* and the latest Harry Potter. It came nowhere near the blockbuster of the following year, *Fifty Shades of Grey.*

After so many years, Luke felt enormous satisfaction at seeing his name on a book cover. In a gesture of defiance, he dedicated the book to Julie, Susie, Carrie and his three grandchildren. Reviews in Britain and Australia were generally enthusiastic and none that were critical or hostile. (Luke could remember a time when *The Times Literary Supplement* had all its reviews written anonymously. The early part of the week in many staffrooms was devoted to guessing the identity of the writers.) He made sure that the Fletchers received signed copies.

PART NINE

Luke

CHAPTER TWENTY-SEVEN

WE WILL ALWAYS HAVE SIDMOUTH

August 2010

A weekend in Sidmouth was part of Luke's family ritual. His parents had always gone there for a break every year. Luke always suspected, as his mother seemed a little skittish about talking about it, that their first visit may have been before they were married. His father's reaction was more robust, echoing the film, *Casablanca,* 'We will always have Sidmouth!' There seemed in reality very little resemblance at all between the world of Rick's café and the Devon seaside resort with its Georgian façade and harbour.

As a child, Luke had always protested – slightly – at going to Sidmouth. Inwardly, he rather enjoyed the pebble beach: eating ice cream on the esplanade; and scoffing fish and chips, wrapped in newspaper. Sidmouth has a reassuring ambience, and from an early age, Luke was allowed to wander the streets away from his parents' gaze. He particularly enjoyed second-hand book shops and in his mid-teens, being tall for his age, he was able to buy several illegal pints without too much difficulty.

The family always stayed at the Royal Glen Hotel, as it had good views and, more importantly, welcomed the family's Labrador, Monty. Luke's parents spent a lot of time chatting in the lounge, and reading newspapers and books; 'unwinding' was the official explanation. However, they also enjoyed a few walks along the Jurassic coastline. One year, Luke had some success catching fish on a boat trip, which the Hotel grilled for him for dinner (he was also allowed wine with meals – an important step to adulthood). However, his enthusiasm did dwindle towards the end of his teenage years and the excuse of 'revising for his exams' was a good let out for his non-attendance.

Luke took Susie to Sidmouth for two reasons: partly, as a kind of nostalgic trip back to his adolescence (he had never got round to taking either of his wives), but mainly because she had burst out laughing, when she saw pictures of Morris dancing. 'I can't believe all those grown men and women wear those ridiculous outfits, going around clashing sticks and ringing bells,' she exclaimed.

Luke could not resist reminding her of the claim of Sir Thomas Beecham. 'Try everything once, except incest and Morris dancing.'

They had a lovely August weekend at the Sidmouth Folk Festival. Unlike some music festivals that can become quite aggressive, the whole atmosphere was calm and gentle. It must be one of the few places, where in concerts the audience on occasions sing along lustily with the performer! Susie's prejudices about Morris dancing were blown away. 'It's beautiful!' she admitted, 'and skilful.' As a repentance gesture, they spent Saturday evening buying and consuming vast amounts of beer with a Morris dance troupe, who explained the various sets. She was impressed by the number of women involved and bought several DVDs of their performances.

They stayed – of course – at the Royal Glen. Luke had not appreciated before that it had royal connections. As a young girl, Queen Victoria had stayed there when it was a private house and had survived an assassination attempt. Her father had lived for a while at Woolbrook Cottage in the town. He caught pneumonia and died. 'Enough history,' proclaimed Susie, 'I want to know more about Morris dancers.'

On the Sunday night, a little tiddly from drinking with yet another Morris dancing troupe, they rolled back to the hotel. 'I have had a lovely time,' whispered Susie.

Saturday, 7th August 2010, 11.50pm

Luke, fast asleep, suddenly fell out of bed with a scream that echoed throughout the hotel. He felt as if he had been hit by lightning and had a horrible, surging pain in his whole body. 'For God's sake, I'm dying,' he yelled, 'get an ambulance.' He was unable to focus and felt as if he were spinning totally out of control. Apart from the lightning strike, he subsequently felt no pain, but could not stop vomiting.

Luke felt this was a bizarre out of body experience, which he was watching from at a short distance. His jumbled thoughts were that he was dying; he grasped Susie's hand and screamed a confused declaration of love. There was a loud whooshing sound in his ears and the spinning feeling got worse.

Luke felt a pulling sensation to the right but his body wanted to stay left. The spinning feeling grew worse and he clung to the bed with the desperation of a drowning man. He tried to explain to the ambulance crew that his eyes felt crossed, but he could hardly speak. Luke lost control of his bladder and he was drenched in sweat; he was soaked from head to toe.

The hotel foyer was empty and Luke was carried down the main stairs to the ambulance. 'It looks as though he has had a stroke, 'explained the senior medic to Susie. She could recall none of the classic warning signs: face drooping, vertigo, double vision, arm weakening and speech difficulty.

The hospital was only 20 miles away and there was little traffic but it was a nightmare journey. By now Luke was unable to speak. His face was tingling and his body was limp and sweating, vomiting continued uncontrollably. He clung to the bed with a manic intensity. 'Will he be all right?' asked a distraught Susie. 'Difficult to say,' said the Senior Medic, 'the next few days will be crucial.'

CHAPTER TWENTY-EIGHT

A VERY ROCKY ROAD

August – September 2010

Luke remembered nothing of the next few days. He drooped pitifully on the bed, as if it were a life line. Susie stayed with him until she was told kindly, 'Get some sleep. He's going to be all right but he's going to need you to be fully fit.'

Luke began to come round but to a very strange world. Horrible thoughts crowded in. 'Will I die tonight? Will I have another attack? Will I ever get out of here?' He was still off balance and very dizzy. His eyes could not focus and he kept seeing spots and flashes.

After ten days, Luke was suffering a nightmare of different experiences: unable to control right leg; memory loss; an inability to focus, lack of balance; and very poor appetite. Words seem to stick in his throat. 'I am a total fucking mess,' he spat out after yet another breakfast, when he could not feed himself.

But there was something worse. For the first time in his life, Luke was depressed, very depressed. He felt as if a ton weight had settled on him. He tried not to cry when Susie was there but he could not help himself. 'I want to go home,' he moaned, 'I hate it here.'

Luke seemed to have relapsed into childhood. He had to be helped with everything. A nurse, with a strong Irish accent and a no-nonsense attitude, bathed, dressed, and fed him. She had little time for his moaning. 'Look around,' she told him crisply, 'count yourself lucky. You're going to live and, if you are a good boy, you have a chance of recovery and a semi normal life. Not all of them here are in the same boat.'

Thoughts about death haunted him, however much, he pushed them away. How he wished he could banish his agnostic uncertainties. He had always envied his mother's simple faith. He always felt that her idea of heaven was a deluxe Women's Institute AGM with a few chosen men in attendance. Whenever he raised any doctrinal point, he was always told, 'no idea, dear, but I am sure God has got it worked out.'

The certainties of some of his university colleagues' atheism meant a final permanent dark hole but it least it was definite. The process of dying frightened him, nearly as much as what happened next. He was visited by the hospital's counsellor and priests from the various denominations. The most helpful was the Anglican vicar, who did not mention God at all but discussed progress in the Test Match.

The next two months were a case of a few steps forward and too many steps back. Progress was slow with a few triumphs: getting to the toilet and back unaided; being able to watch the news and remember most of it; and cutting up his Sunday lunch. He popped a lot of pills. Every day, there were some exercises. Luke never thought that he would spend most of a morning learning to climb stairs again.

There were some difficult realities to face. He would always walk with a pronounced limp with a partially paralysed right side. Perhaps worst of all; he would never be able to write with his right hand, as his fingers could not grip and his arm had lost its sense of control.

The physiotherapist began to set increasingly difficult goals: picking up a range of objects from the floor; reading things at a distance; and getting dressed without help. Luke looked around the ward and saw that he had indeed been lucky. Some remained permanently bed-bound and were often fed by tube. Worryingly, a bed would become empty without explanation.

Luke faced his final appraisal ten weeks after he was admitted. 'He must have done this so many times before,' he thought, as he and Susie looked over the senior surgeon's desk. On the table was a prominently displayed picture of a wife, three children and a Spaniel. 'Do you want the good news or the bad news?' asked the consultant. Without waiting for a reply, he continued, 'you are going to be able to live a fairly normal life. There's no reason why you shouldn't be able to draw the old age pension. You need to look around the ward and see that you have been lucky. Not all will leave and others will have severe mobility problems. Admittedly, I can confirm that you will always have a limp and restricted use of your right arm. Probably no more tennis! As you have been finding out, you will have to make some everyday adjustments in areas, such as dressing and tying your shoe laces. I have had several cases where patients have learnt to write with their left hand. One of them said that his writing had improved. We won't say goodbye because we want to see you for an occasional check-up.'

Luke slowly limped around the beds and shook hands with most of the ward's patients. 'I'm going to have to get used to shaking hands with my left hand,' he muttered. One of the beds commented bitterly, 'at least you can use one hand.' He broke NHS protocol and gave the Irish nurse a big hug (he found out that she was Aoife O'Keefe) and then a kiss on the cheek. 'Ah, there's nothing wrong with you,' she exclaimed and patted him in a sisterly fashion on the shoulder.

Luke felt like he had hit a road block in the next few weeks. Never the most dexterous of men, he stumbled around the downstairs furniture with the occasional burst of swearing, when he hit something. He needed a daily helping hand for so many simple chores, ranging from tin opening to tying parcels. Some tasks, such as driving a car or mowing the lawn, were history.

His efforts to write with his left hand were a depressing failure, rescued in part by new technology. He splashed out on a dictation to text computer and, after a few false starts, achieved a degree of competence. (There were a few minor mishaps, when the machine mistook churchyard for Churchill.)

The biggest change was in his relationship with Susie. He tried not to treat her as a nursemaid but she did have to take on extra tasks, ranging from carving the Sunday roast to filling out forms. He realised that he was often grumpy but was not always able to check it. Sometimes Susie was short with him and bad tempered. Trips and treats became fewer and were less spontaneous.

But it was the saga of the coffee pot that brought things to a head. Increasingly, Luke's day depended on his first cup and he was overanxious in pushing the plunger of the cafetiere. Obeying the rule that dictates that dropped vessels of liquid are always full; the steaming coffee drenched the floor, table cloth, wall and curtains. Something inside Luke simply snapped. He picked up the pot and smashed it into smithereens, the glass going everywhere. He grabbed the breakfast plates and threw then as far as he could. He stumbled around the kitchen breaking everything he could grasp – pictures, glasses and vases. Only Susie's screaming stopped him in his tracks. It was the first time that he had seen her cry.

'I can't stand it,' she sobbed, 'I feel trapped. Of course, I want to help you but you are so bloody ungrateful. I don't just want to be a nursemaid.

'And there's another thing. Commuting between here and Australia is not going to work long-term. It's not like flying to France or Spain; it's the other side of the world. I'm not sure if I'm an Aussie or a Pom any longer.'

Late September 2010

Eventually, Luke sat Susie down, when they had both calmed a little, with yet another bottle of Hardy's Red. 'We've got to talk,' he said, 'we can't go on like this. I cannot go on expecting you to wait on me hand and foot. You've got your own life and there is also Australia. I need to make myself more self-reliant within the boundaries that I have.

'I think you need to go back to Oz and take a break from me for a while. You need to decide if this is worth the candle. Don't write or text.'

Susie did demur for a while but a few days later, she left with a large suitcase and a one-way ticket. 'I need to clear my head,' she explained.

Luke became a creature of habit. He struggled out of bed at 8 o'clock and endured a masterpiece of tangles to get dressed. Breakfast had been laid out the afternoon before by Sylvia, his newly acquired Polish daily. His day seemed to resolve around the news: 9, 1 and 6.

The biggest wrench was selling the car. There was no Susie to drive it and it took up a lot of room in an overcrowded garage. It did not help that a local sale meant that he saw the car almost every other day. 'If he cheerily waves at me once more and smirks with a thumbs up,' thought Luke, 'I will shove the MOT certificate where it hurts most.'

His horizons shrank: the village shop (central focus of gossip), the mobile library and the community hall (the venue for the local film club). His occasional trips to town had to be carefully orchestrated with resort to helping hands and bus timetables.

Luke felt himself disconnecting. He saw virtually anybody and avoided answering the phone. He gave up on Facebook. He longed to phone or contact Susie but felt that he must stick to their agreement – no contact.

He felt jumbled and confused and, for the first time in his life, he had no long-term goal.

'You're a bloody idiot,' pronounced an exasperated Amelia on a weekend visit, 'you let her go without any real heart to heart. How many times have I got to tell you that woman is gold dust. You should have never let her go back to Australia. I can't believe that you were so dim-witted as to suggest it.'

Henry's suggestion was a little more low key. 'You need a dog,' he pronounced.

'Any particular breed?' asked Luke ironically. 'What do you have in mind? Labrador? Corgi?'

'Anything that gets you out of the house. Gets you moving. Gives some structure to your life. Meet some people dog-walking. Good for exercise. Take you out of yourself.'

Luke did not see himself – however depressed – as a dog owner but he did take up another of Henry's suggestions, helping at the village primary school. 'Your local primary is bound to want people to volunteer at breaktime and lending a hand to over-worked teachers.'

October – December 2010

Luke had no idea of what primary teaching really involved. He found the experience both exhilarating and daunting. His offer of help was gratefully received. 'We need a bloke around the place,' explained the Head, 'we are all women at the moment.'

All the initials after his name counted for nothing and, despite teaching experience, he still had to undergo a security check. His disability meant that he could not help with football or cricket. The thing he enjoyed the most was reading out loud; his *Hound of the Baskervilles* with local accents and atmospheric sounds was a big hit.

Luke was enthralled by the energy and enthusiasm of the classes. He became very aware of social problems; so many children had only one parent, usually a mother, in residence. He admired the commitment of the young staff, whose overwhelming ambition seemed to be making learning fun.

His involvement drew him for the first time more into the community. He ran the PTA Quiz Night as the MC and the deviser of the questions. He even got invited, occasionally, to class birthday parties. He experienced that essential part of school life – the pick up at 3.30pm, a major centre for gossip.

His acceptance boosted his morale and gave him increased confidence.

Luke bonded with one ten-year-old, Arthur – who, despite efforts by the staff, was always an isolated presence on the playground. His stammer and awkward manner seemed to cut him off from the rest. Luke suggested that Arthur help him at reading sessions by turning the pages, something he found difficult. It seemed to work, to a degree, and it was good to see Arthur becoming a little more integrated.

Friday, 21st December 2010

'It has been a better day,' thought Luke. The school's Christmas play, despite being a cliché was a fun cliché. One of the Kings in best panto tradition had picked his nose, as he had presented his gift. The obvious delight of the players and audience was palatable and ahead lay holidays, family time and presents. Luke had been given a lift by Virgin Mary's mum and her parental beam lit up her whole face. 'You were wonderful,' enthused Luke of Virgin Mary, her mother needed no convincing.

Luke noticed that he had left the lights on in the sitting room. He had put up no decorations and sent no cards. Henry and Amelia had offered to put him up over Christmas but he had declined. Luke felt like a party pooper and did not feel convivial.

He reached for the key but noticed that the front door was unlocked. He opened the sitting room door to be confronted by two figures sitting on the sofa in the corner.

'Hello, Luke,' said Susie.

'Hello, Dad,' said Carrie.

PART TEN

Reconciliation

CHAPTER TWENTY-NINE

CATCH UP

Friday, 21st December 2010

Everybody started talking at once. Luke got out a bottle of Cava, heated up some sausage rolls and cleared the table. It was going to be a long night.

Susie explained that, like Luke, she had wanted to phone or email a thousand times, even sometimes once or twice in an hour. The trip to Australia superficially had gone well; the family farm was in an up period. She did not check on Greg! 'The brothers agreed that Carrie should be left alone but were saddened by being cut off. They agreed that, 'Mum and Dad would have wanted to know if she were well.'

Life in Brisbane seemed flat. 'I missed you and could not get started. I appreciated that you had given me time to think things over but my mind was made up. I put the flat on the market and it is sold.'

Luke interjected, 'I've had a lot of time to think too. I have missed you desperately. I promise that I will be more patient. I've been worked on my mobility and am getting a little more coordinated.'

Susie continued at breakneck speed, words tumbling out. 'I could not leave Carrie any longer. I decided to go to Hydra and somehow arrange a meeting.'

Carrie interrupted. 'It was a cunning idea getting Giorgos on board. He was the only one who could talk me round.'

'Yes, it was a bit of luck. I waited for him where the fishing boats came in on the quay. I nabbed him on the way home and sat him in a café for a ten-minute talk that took nearly two hours. Luckily, time is more flexible in Greece.

'Greeks are great ones for families and when I described to him how Luke had a stroke and was desperate to see his daughter and grandchildren. He began to crumble and I noticed tears in his eyes. I emphasised that Luke had had no idea of Carrie's existence till a few years' ago, since then he had been desperate to see her and his grandchildren.'

'It was pretty sneaky, watching us on Facebook,' commented Carrie.

'Yes, but it showed how desperate we were to see you all.'

'How did you two make it up?' asked Luke.

'Giorgos bought Susie to the café and sat us down at a table out of the way. Within in a few minutes, we were both in tears.'

Susie continued, 'I explained that we were all so concerned but we could and should have done more. Julie and I were always very close, but I felt so helpless.'

Luke produced another bottle of Cava and the conversation became even more animated. Carrie explained, 'Susie stayed with us for six weeks and she was great. She got on like a house on fire with the kids and did a bit of waiting in the evenings. She even learnt a few Greek words and phrases.

'She was brilliant at sorting out the books. Both Giorgos and I are a little chaotic when it comes to money. Susie introduced a proper system that we could all understand. We both went on a trip to Athens and got an up-to-date cash register that has been a great help in getting us more organised. We are really set up for the tax man this time!

'My heart went out at the thought of Dad suffering a stroke and I couldn't not harden my heart and not see him.' Luke relished the use of the word, 'Dad.'

'And we have both made a decision. We have decided that we are all going back to Hydra.'

At about two o'clock, Luke showed Carrie to the spare room. Susie noted that he had become more adept at undressing.

'It's just as well that I have still got my left arm to cuddle you,' he murmured. 'Welcome back. I have missed you desperately. There has not been a day when I haven't thought of you.'

They both fell into a trance-like sleep.

Tuesday, 18th January 2011

Luke sat on the café's balcony and lit a cigarette. (Susie now allowed him five a day and he found that he did not require much will power to stick to it.) 'It had,' he reflected, 'been the best Christmas ever.' Local traditions and customs had entranced him and had drawn him in with their warmth and sincerity.

It had started when Giorgos and his crew had decorated the boats with lights and decorations, and pictures of the nativity. Soon all the other boats in the harbour were similarly decorated, with each one trying to outdo the others. Britain seemed very remote; he had come across a several days' old *Daily Mail* with pictures of over a hundred deaths at a religious festival in Kerela in India. Here, religion seemed warmth and friendly; Luke had no difficulty, despite his agnosticism, in joining in with the singing and chanting of the Orthodox Church.

'It is just as well that I have a sweet tooth,' thought Luke, as he was plied with Greek Christmas sweets. He particularly liked *melomakarona* and *kourabiedes*, sugar coated biscuits. He also became partial to *diples* made from syrupy pastry.

Carrie showed him another Greek tradition. She decorated a shallow wooden bowl with a piece of wire suspended across the rim. A sprig of basil was wrapped around a wooden cross and hung from the wire. The bowl contained water to keep the basil alive and fresh. Once a day, someone, usually Carrie, dipped the cross and basil into some holy water, and sprinkled the water in every room.

'This keeps the *kallikantzroi,* bad sprits, away. They only appear during the 12-day period from Christmas to Epiphany,' she explained. 'They come from the middle of the earth and get into people's houses through the chimney. They do things like putting out fires and making the milk go sour. We must keep a fire burning to help scare them off, and burning old shoes is also a good deterrent.'

It had all started on the morning of Christmas Eve with local children, including Luke's three grandchildren, singing carols to the noise of metal triangles and drums. Carrie came down to the door and gave out sweets. Luke was expecting presents to be handed out on Christmas Day but the Greek tradition is to give presents on 1st January, the feast of Saint Basil. The Saint is depicted as an old man with a white beard and he seems to have merged a good deal in popular imagination with Santa Claus.

There were a lot of family and local traditions. On New Year's Eve, Giorgos stood outside the house with a pomegranate, which he broke on the door step. 'The seeds of the fruit are meant to bring happiness and health to the family,' explained Carrie.

Giorgos' mother, Sophia, a formidable matriarch figure, baked a St Basil Cake, called *Vasilopita,* which was served at midnight on New Year's Eve. When he bit his piece, Luke felt something hard. A coin is always inserted and the finder is meant to be lucky for the rest of the year. (Luke closed his eyes and wished that the visit would be a success.) Sophia cut the cake into pieces. 'The first piece is for Christ; the second for the Virgin Mary, the third for poor people and the fourth for the household,' she explained. 'The family get it in order of age and seniority.'

All the tables from the restaurant were put together and elaborately decorated (Luke noted a Union Jack and the Australian flag). Carrie and Sophia served a mammoth pork joint, roasted over an open spit, accompanied by a spinach and cheese pie, salads and vegetables. Luke kept glancing at Carrie and was filled with pride at how she fitted in and how obviously happy she was. Susie gave his hand a squeeze. 'I'm loving this,' she said.

'Me too,' replied Luke.

'A cliché is a truth that has been too often repeated,' commented Luke. 'But children *do* make Christmas.' He had not realised how, deep in the recess of his being, how much he had missed children and grandchildren. They were not angels. There were a few squabbles over Christmas but these were easily sorted out. He had spent a lot of time selecting presents and they were met with squeals of delight: an Olympiacos football shirt for Dimitris; yellow football boots for Nicholas; and a special nurse's outfit for Maria's teddy bear. Several times over Christmas, Luke remembered the chain of events that had bought him to the island and how no historian could have predicted them and how much luck had played a part. Sometimes, he found it difficult to believe himself. There was only one present that he could possibly give to Susie, Carrie and Giorgos, a *mati*, the Greek good luck eye.

Hydra also gave Luke the opportunity to come to grudging terms with his disability. The sunshine helped.

He did not have to wear so many clothes and sandals were so much easier to manage. He loved basking in the warm sunshine and he found movement easier.

The attitude of the Greeks was another bonus. He hardly had to wait any time at all by the side of the road, supported by his stick, for somebody to offer to help or to carry something for him. The pace of Greek life with its absence of rush and bother suited him, and he found his body becoming more relaxed. He loved the fact that the only vehicles allowed on the island were to collect the rubbish. His daily routines became more established.

Luke relished his time with Carrie and soon began to realise that she was a chip off the old block. Occasionally, a gesture or a look would remind him of Julie. She was very direct and had an ample dose of the Aussie distrust of bullshit. 'Would I have coped with Julie as a long- term partner?' he wondered. He admitted to himself that he was totally biased, but he did admire the loving family atmosphere that Carrie had created.

A local mystery was revealed to Luke: why so much of a Greek Christmas involves rich food. 'Many Greeks go on a strict fast before Christmas,' explained Carrie. 'It's one of the few Greek customs that I've not adopted.'

Luke loved fitting in with the ordinary details of everyday life. He went to Nicholas and Maria's primary school and read a story in English and showed everybody where in England he came from. When the sea was calm, he went out with Giorgos and his crew. He enjoyed chatting to the visitors to the café, a steady stream of which were British.

New Year's Day was a very special occasion. Presents were given out during the day with lots of hugs and kisses (Luke found himself embracing cousins and aunts he had never seen before). He noticed with approval that bedtimes seemed to be very flexible, indeed almost non-existent. There was a lot of carol singing; Luke was impressed that every other person played a musical instrument. The family had a tradition of *Bounamathes*, giving money and more gifts to children and wishing them a happy new year. Giorgos appeared to be related to half the island. Luke did not feel at all self-conscious in joining in the dancing but at his own pace.

He was greatly touched that Sophia had baked him another round of *Christopsomo*, Christ's bread, as he had admired it so much over Christmas. It was a small round bread, flavoured with cinnamon, orange and cloves. The top was decorated with a cross. Luke asked for the recipe but was told – half in jest – that 'only a Greek mother can make it.'

The day had begun with *Pothariko*, when Dimitris, as the eldest child, was the first person to enter the house with his right foot. It must be the right foot to bring the household good luck. Luke admired the Greek notion of Christmas, very much centred around family and friends, and not the television. Greeks seemed also much more involved in what was meant to be a Christian festival.

The festivities ended on 6th. January, Epiphany, with a ceremony that was of great significance in the fishing community. A large crowd, gathered around the harbour made up of locals with a sprinkling of visitors. The local priest, with a magnificent flowing beard, said prayers, and then threw a cross, which he had blessed, into the sea. A horde of young men dived in and a neighbour's son emerged with it – minutes later – with a triumphant grin. 'That boat will get a lot of fish this year,' exclaimed Carrie.

Tuesday, 25th January 2011

Luke was able to spend a lot of time with Carrie once the Christmas celebrations were over. Life at the café was a little more subdued, waiting for spring. The media was full of news from Egypt, where the government was under pressure from a protesting mob.

They got into the habit of chatting every morning. (The meetings only reinforced Luke's belief that the British seem incapable of making really good coffee.) 'I think part of my reason for being against any contact was that, subconsciously, I hated you,' she confessed. 'Mum and Ritchie seemed increasingly to loath each other most of the time and your name was always being dragged into their rows. I was the obvious bit of evidence that Mum had been with somebody else.

'I think she built you up into some kind of idealised fantasy figure, as a contrast to Ritchie. Your name was often thrown about. Mum's death made things even worse. His dislike of me intensified. I tried to hide when they argued and fought and, when she died, I tried blacking out, when he started to punch and hit me.

'The feeling ups and the groping were not really about sex but his anger at the situation. I was also like Mum. I refused to back down. One day, he tried to rape me and I fought back with everything I had. I punched, scratched and pummelled him but that only seemed to encourage him. I told him that if it ever happened again, I would report him to the police.

'I planned my escape over a couple of years. I put aside money without him knowing. I got my own passport. I picked a week, when he was away at some cattle fair. I left a note, saying I was gone for good. To be honest, I think he was probably relieved.

'I had no plans; it was exhilarating. I hitched across Europe and arrived in Piraeus. I met Giorgos at a café, where I was waitressing. He was there getting equipment for his boat and for a wedding of a relative. He wanted some help in the café, someone who could speak English and some French. I fell for, and married, the boss. I have no interest in pursuing Greg for the property or getting any money out of him. I want to blot out all memories of the place.'

PART ELEVEN

Third Time Lucky?

CHAPTER THIRTY

A VERY BLUNT EMAIL

Saturday, 12th February 2011

Even by Amelia's bulldozer standards, it was a very blunt email.

> To: Luke
>
> From: Amelia
>
> Topic: What are you doing, you dozy idiot?
>
> Date: 12th February - two days before Valentine's Day
>
> Luke, I will kick you where it hurts most, if you do not propose to Susie in two days' time. Everybody thinks she is far too good for you. She's bright, sexy and kind. It is pretty obvious that the poor, deluded woman is in love with you. She has sold her house and is prepared to put up with the English winter and you hobbling around. I can't see her, however, ever cheering for England in any sporting contest with Australia - there are limits.
>
> For fuck's sake, get your finger out and ask her. Henry agrees with all of this and will insist on being best man. He has promised not to say, even after a lot of beers, 'third time, lucky.'
>
> You really are off the Christmas card list this time for ever, if you don't do the decent thing. And make a proper job of it; none of this out of the corner of your mouth stuff, 'I

don't suppose, you might consider' nonsense. Come right out and give her the full barrelled treatment, but make it romantic.

Good luck and remember, I can kick very hard. Best love, Amelia XXXX

Luke emailed back: 'Already organised. Ring even bought.'

CHAPTER THIRTY-ONE

A GREAT DAY

Saturday, 18th June 2011

It was, everybody agreed, a great wedding. Luke had reflected several times in the past on his track record. His first was in a church; solely for the benefit of his mother and mother-in-law. The second was a clandestine one with two witnesses, commandeered from the Registry Office's cleaning staff. 'Thank you, sir,' said the senior one, as she pocketed a ten-pound note. 'It's not the first that I've done – a nice little earner.' The fact that the ceremony and the party this time was in their own garden made it special.

Everybody came or had a very good excuse. A strong Scottish contingent made the journey, including two young nephews, who got rather sick on some sneaked beers but hardly anybody noticed. Two of Susie's brothers and their wives travelled from Australia and made it part of a European holiday. Carrie came with the children, who were delighted to be part of the ceremony. Grigios stayed to mind the restaurant. Sophia sent some *karidopita,* a cake with almonds, which is often served at Greek weddings. A handful of former colleagues from the university announced that they 'would not have missed it for the world.' There were, mercifully, no speeches but a very large and long lunch and dancing to the early hours.

Several villagers also came, including the postmistress. 'I go to all the local weddings,' she explained after several glasses of wine.

To calm any pre-wedding nerves, Luke and Susie had sat down a few days before with a bottle of Hardys Red.

The decision on the honeymoon was easy and took only two sips of wine – Hydra.

'Everything that is dear to me, apart from you, is in Hydra': proclaimed Luke. 'I think we should also settle there long term.'

'A beaut idea' agreed Susie, 'I can keep an eye on Carrie and help in the café. The weather and no cars are so much better for your health. It's not quite half way between England and Australia but it would cut the cost of the air flights.'

'I have already got the estate agents brochures,' confessed Luke.

About the Author

John Kirkaldy was born of an Anglo-Scottish father and a Norwegian mother in Kashmir in 1947, one of the last children of Imperial India. His father was a junior Army officer, trying to cope with one of the biggest forced migrations in history – the territorial division between India and Pakistan – and the source of many large-scale human tragedies. Kashmir is still a highly disputed area, the cause of three wars and endless border disputes, coupled with a Kashmiri independence movement.

His upbringing was a typical one of the post World War Two run down of Empire with three-year family postings to Manchester, Burma (now Myanmar), Germany, Hampshire (where he picked up a life-long support for that county in cricket and Southampton in football) and the North East. As a Gunner family, it was resolved not to retire to Salisbury Plain but fate decreed otherwise.

John was educated at Tonbridge, the LSE and the Universities of the West Indies and New South Wales. He has taught in schools, colleges and universities in Britain, Jamaica and Australia. He was an Open University tutor for 38 years.

He lasted one round on the TV quiz show, *The Weakest Link,* and has had to endure the humiliation of endless repeats.

This is John's first novel but he has been writing for most of his life. He has contributed to four anthologies on Irish history and politics, and published numerous journal articles. He has written for magazines as varied as the *New Statesman* and *The Lady* and for newspapers, ranging from the *Mail on Sunday* to *the Independent*. In the mid-70s, he was Australian correspondent for the *THES* and *TES*, writing regular articles on education in that country. He hosted for several years a programme on education on local radio. He was part of course teams, writing and researching, for four OU TV series. He has won several awards for short stories. He has been a book reviewer for *Books Ireland* for over 40 years.

He kept secret to generations of his students, as he urged them to make best use of any gap year or time between study, that he had himself done the world's worst example. He did several months in the City of London, as a trainee accountant; a numbingly boring experience with a dress code worse than school. On retirement, he tried to make amends: took a year off; visited fourteen countries, worked in three; and was a volunteer on a project for Indian women and girls from disadvantaged backgrounds. Very stupidly, he also did a bungee jump, when in New Zealand. The advice here is simple: DON'T. He wrote a travel book on his experiences: *I've Got a Metal Knee: A 70-Year-Old's Gap Year.*